OUR BABY STEPS

From being pregnant to becoming parent

AMAN SHROFF

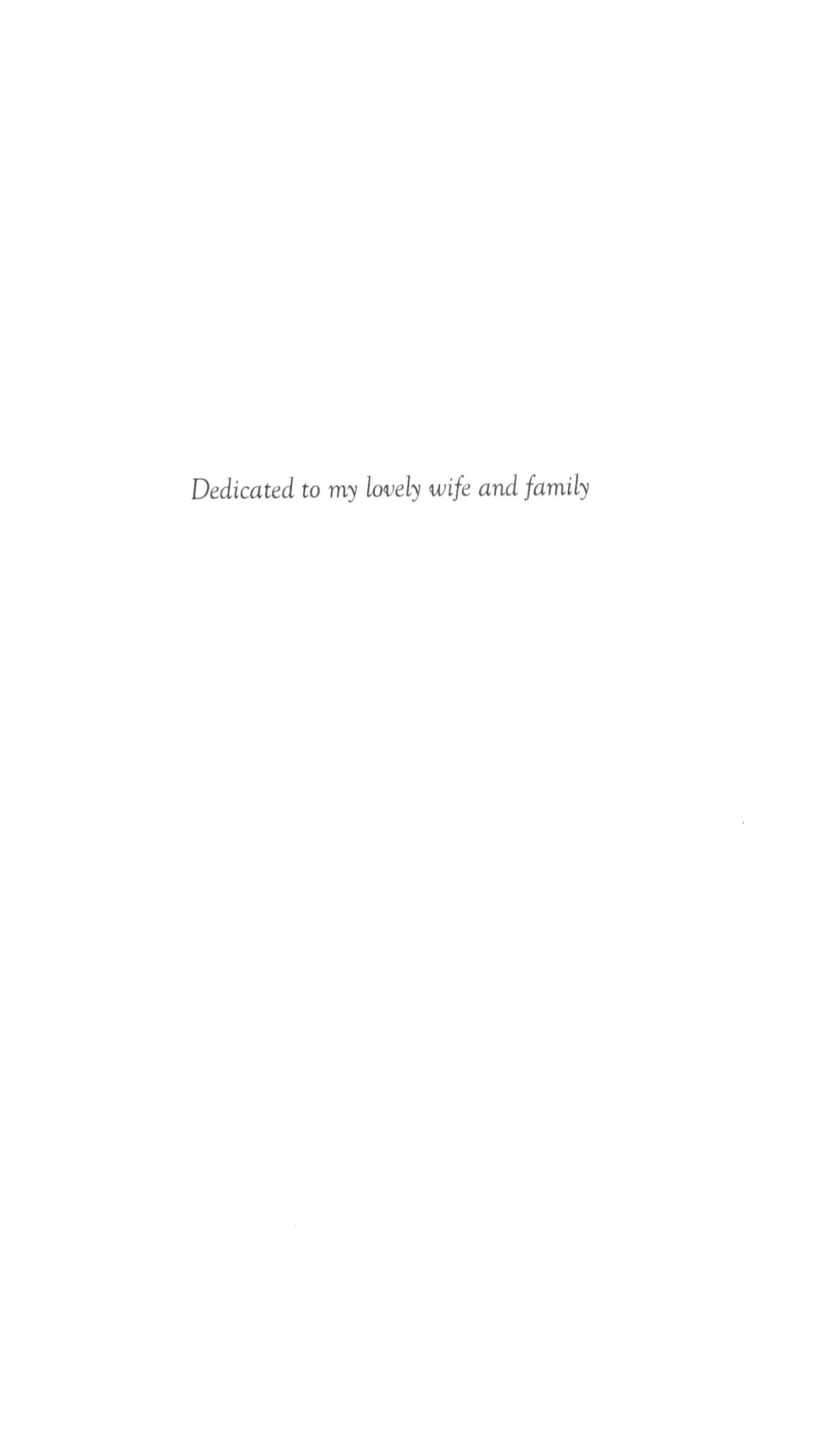

Dedicated to my lovely wife and family

Author's Note

Writing *Our Baby Steps* has been one of the most intimate and fulfilling journeys of my life. *It's* a not-so-fictional narrative that explores the emotional ups and downs, unpredictability, small joys and how life changes with two pink lines.

Our Baby Steps is not a pregnancy handbook. It doesn't offer medical advice or perfect answers—because every pregnancy, every relationship, and every journey to parenthood is different.

To anyone reading this—whether you're a new parent, an expectant one, or simply someone in love with life's little details—I hope this book makes you smile, pause, and perhaps remember your own journey.

— Aman Shroff

FIRST MONTH

Are We Pregnant?

"Purvi, it's already 5 PM, and we need to leave by 6, as there's no bus after that. Where are you?" I asked, trying to keep my voice calm despite the rising panic.

"I know, but they're not letting me leave. I WILL MISS MY TRAIN!" she screamed—a rare outburst from my usually calm wife.

Purvi, my wife, works at a bank in Umaria, while I work for an IT company. However, since I'm currently working from home, I'm staying with her.

"Why? What happened? Don't worry, we still have some time," I said, trying to soothe her.

"I'll come and explain everything. I just need to finish this never-ending work." She hung up abruptly.

I stood there, phone in hand, feeling utterly clueless. The bags were still unpacked. I have never been good at packing—honestly, I have never really tried, as Purvi always handled it like a pro. But I tried to gather some of my clothes, stuffing them haphazardly into a bag. We had two bags: one for her clothes and another for mine and our essentials.

For a three-day trip, I figured I could manage with one pair of blue jeans, a capri for sleeping, three shirts or t-shirts, and one for nightwear. As I packed, a nagging worry occupied my mind: would we even be able to go? Our tickets were still in tatkal waiting list, positions 13 and 14.

My thoughts were interrupted by a call. "I just left," Purvi said, her frustration evident, her breaths quick.

"Are you coming to Chat Corner? It will be easy to get an Auto for Bus Stand from there" she continued.

Umaria is a small town with limited transportation options. Ola and Uber don't operate here. At best, you can find an auto rickshaw from specific areas to get around.

"But we still need to pack..." I felt useless.

"You didn't... Okay, no problem. Let me come, and we'll pack quickly."

"Hmm, okay," I agreed, hanging up. I tried to do as much as I could before she arrived, checking the train status frequently. It was right on time—15-20 minutes late, which is considered on time in Indian Railways. I kept refreshing the IRCTC page for our ticket status, hoping for a miracle as the chart was supposed to be prepared by 5 PM.

I gathered essential items like a toothbrush, power bank, and water bottle, placing them together. I heard the gate open, and there she was, consoling Madhu, our neighbour and dear friend, who was in tears.

"Madhu, what's wrong?" I asked, but Purvi shook her head, signalling it wasn't the right time to ask.

Madhu and Vibha are our neighbours, and they both also work at a bank.

"They're all selfish people. We can't help much. Just let me know if you need anything," Purvi murmured as Madhu went to her room.

I quickly closed our door as Purvi entered. "Poor Madhu, she was going home and had a train at 5, but her heartless colleagues didn't let her leave. She was so sad. Anyway, let's pack."

"What? Are we going or not?" She asked, looking at my calm, quiet face.

"I don't know. The chart hasn't been prepared yet."

She sighed deeply. "Now what? Should I check for other trains? Or another destination if not Varanasi?"

"I checked. Nothing is available for Varanasi."

"I just want to go somewhere. I can't stay in this village on a 3-day holiday," she said.

"Hey! Mathura's ticket is available for Premium Tatkal. Should I book that?" she asked excitedly.

I was still unsure what to do. "See, I've already told everyone at work that we have tickets and we're going. Even my senior got excited and planned to go to Varanasi with his family after I told him about the great 'Dev Deepawali' Festival. And now we won't be going," she said in disappointment.

"We can go to Mathura or Varanasi. I'm also not sure," I said, feeling the pressure.

"The last bus to reach Katni railway station from this village is at 6. We only have 30 minutes. Tell me, should I pack for Mathura or Varanasi?" she demanded.

"Mathura's ticket is available, right? Let's go there, let me book it.

"Okay, I'll start packing."

I glanced at my phone and froze. "Shit—it's gone."

"What?"

"The ticket. It's not available anymore."

"What the hell, yaar. It's all because of my Colleagues. If they'd let me leave early, we could have made a decision. Now, forget it. I don't want to go anywhere."

"We can still go to Varanasi. Quickly, pack. We have to leave," I said, sensing her disappointment.

"Are you sure?" she asked.

"Yes, yes."

She quickly gathered things from the shelf, folded her clothes, and, as expected, took out all my clothes from my bag, folding them neatly and arranging them properly. She freshened up, got changed, tied her hair back, and got ready. I filled the bottles, put on my shirt and jeans, grabbed my wallet, and within 20 minutes, we were ready to go.

"Did you check the lights?" she asked.

"Yes."

"And also turn off the gas regulator, please," she requested.

"Okay, done. Can we go now?" I asked, turning it off.

"Yeah, yeah, almost done. Just let me go to the washroom," she said, heading there.

"Okay, I'm out, wearing my shoes, and I've kept both bags here. Just come," I said.

"Ha, let's g—" She paused, looking at me. I was sitting there, disappointed, with one shoe on and the other in my hand.

"What?" she asked.

I gathered the courage to look at her and nodded. "Tickets not confirmed."

She was utterly disappointed and sat beside me. "Chart prepared?" she asked in a low tone.

"Hmm, 11-12 waiting," I said.

She was almost in tears and was about to cry as she got up to go inside the room. Then she turned back as I said, "But leave it. We will go in General. I mean, can we? If you want to go? Should we go?"

She turned her back. "Leave it. Let's not go anywhere now. I DON'T WANT TO GO ANYWHERE NOW," she said, resigned to our bad luck.

I removed my shoe and went inside to console her as she came out of the washroom.

I looked at her, her shoulders slumped, and for a second, I hated how helpless I felt. As if a simple train ticket held the weight of our happiness.

"Sorry," I said.

"Why are you sorry?" she asked.

"I... I... don't know," I stammered.

"Don't worry. We'll enjoy here. We'll watch series, movies, and eat well. Let's cook biryani today. And I'll try making noodles, the one shown in Naruto," I said, trying to cheer her up.

"Hmm."

"Okay, come, let's go to the market," I suggested, to bring the veggies and masala for biryani, trying to cheer her mood.

I changed into my regular clothes, and she did the same. She was very silent, which was understandable. I didn't push her much.

"Shall we?" I asked.

"Hmm," she murmured, going to the kitchen for some water.

I grabbed my phone and the door keys. She got out and wore her slippers.

"Should we invite Madhu? I think we should. She's also sad. Let's invite her," I suggested.

"I'm not in the mood to talk to anyone," she said.

"Arey, just go and ask her."

"Hmm," she agreed reluctantly.

She knocked on Madhu's door and called out, 'Madhu?'

Madhu opened the door, smiling. Before we could ask, she explained, "I'm going home."

"What? Wow, but how?" Purvi asked, trying to show her happiness for her.

"I called my dad and narrated the whole situation. But to our surprise, there's one train which is 15 hours late, so it will reach here by 11-12 PM. I can still make it home. Hurray!" she said, unable to contain her excitement.

"Oh wow, that's some luck," Purvi said.

"But wait, what about you?" Madhu asked.

Purvi looked at me. "Tickets didn't get confirmed," I said.

"Ohh!" Madhu said, still happy.

"Anyway, we were thinking of making biryani. Would you like to join?" Purvi asked.

"Okay, sure," Madhu replied without hesitation.

"We're going to get some groceries and items from the market and will be back soon," Purvi said.

"Okay, let me know if you need any help," Madhu replied.

"I thought talking to Madhu would cheer her up, but it backfired. She seemed even sadder now.

The dialogue from *3 Idiots* came to mind: '*Pata nahi Rancho, tumhare saath aisa kyun hota hai.*'"

We didn't speak much on our way to the market. I glanced at Purvi a few times, hoping to catch her eye and start a conversation.

"So, what all do we need?" I asked, attempting to break the silence.

"Biryani Masala and Coconut for Salan, I guess, we mostly have all the veggies" she replied shortly, not looking at me.

At the store, I spotted some packaged ramen and got an idea. "Hey, how about I make Naruto-style noodles?" I asked, holding up the packet.

She raised an eyebrow. "Do you even know how to make them?"

"How hard can it be? Boil noodles, add toppings, and voilà!" I said confidently.

"Right" she said with a faint smile, moving ahead to pick up ingredients for the biryani.

When we returned, the kitchen became a bustling hub of activity. Purvi started with her preparations, her focus unwavering. I decided to experiment with my noodles.

Madhu arrived shortly after, "So, what's cooking? Need any help" she asked, looking around.

"Biryani and salan, yes please chop these off" Purvi replied, handing some veggies to Madhu.

"And I'm making Naruto-style noodles," I added proudly.

Madhu raised an eyebrow. "Naruto-style noodles? Can't wait!"

As the biryani filled the kitchen with its tantalizing aroma, I struggled with my noodles. They didn't look anything like the ones I had seen in anime. The broth was too watery, the noodles overcooked, and the toppings were sliding off.

"Done!" I announced, placing a bowl on the table with a flourish.

Madhu peered at the bowl cautiously.

"Looks can be deceiving," I replied, taking a spoonful. It tasted bland and lacked the flavours I had imagined.

She wrinkled her nose. "I'll pass. That biryani smells much more promising."

Purvi chuckled softly.

"Fine," I said dramatically. "I'll eat it myself. It's... not bad," I lied, forcing another bite.

"Wow Purvi, this smells so good," Madhu said, eagerly taking a plate.

I nodded in agreement. "Yeah, and this is her first time cooking Biryani."

"Let's see if it tastes as good as it smells," she said modestly, sitting down to eat.

And it was delicious. The flavours were rich, perfectly balanced, and the rice was cooked to perfection.

"This is amazing," I said, genuinely impressed, pushing my noodles aside.

Madhu nodded enthusiastically. "Purvi, So good."

Purvi smiled, her earlier quietness replaced by a warmth that lit up her face. "I'm glad you both like it."

We all enjoyed the meal, the earlier silence and awkwardness completely forgotten. The evening ended with full stomachs, light hearts, and a shared sense of company that made the day truly special.

After dinner, Purvi and I went for our daily walk.

"What should we watch?" I asked.

"Anything," she said.

"Series, movies, what?" I asked again.

"Anything is fine," she said.

"Umm, I heard *The Railway Men* is good," I suggested.

"Is it a series?" she asked.

"Yes, on Netflix, about the Bhopal Gas tragedy. Released today," I said.

"Okay, let's watch that," she agreed.

After returning from our walk and finishing our chores, we settled into bed, wrapped in blankets, dimmed the lights, and started watching *The Railway Men*. The series was captivating and kept us hooked, lifting our spirits a bit. We watched until 3 AM, finishing the entire series, and decided to sleep in. But at around 8 AM, her phone rang. It was my sister, Priya, who rarely calls, especially not this early. That's when I woke up too.

"Ha didi," Purvi answered, barely awake.

"Nahi, nahi. Tell me," She replied, probably when Priya asked if she had woken us up.

On a weekend at 8 AM, of course, she had.

Priya wanted to order some haircare product and was inquiring about it. "Yes, I tried that. It is quite good. You can definitely order it," Purvi said.

"Yes, hairfall also seems to have reduced," Purvi replied to something Priya said.

"Okay, didi, sure. Bye."

"After that, I tried to drift back to sleep, but Purvi suddenly shouted, 'It's not fair, yaar!"

"What? Where?" I asked, half-asleep.

"My family! They also went out of town. Only I'm stuck here," Purvi said, showing photos on her family WhatsApp group.

I decided that it was too much sadness. I quickly looked at my phone and checked running trains.

"Purvi, quickly get up and get ready," I said.

"What!"

"Yes, we are also leaving. There's a train in 40 minutes to Katni. Let's go."

"But what will we do there? Where will we go from Katni?" she asked.

"I don't know. Varanasi, it's an 8-9 hour journey, and in daytime we can manage that much. Or Jabalpur. I'm not sure, but we will definitely go somewhere. Just get ready," I said.

"Are you sure?" she asked, with a bit of excitement.

"Yes! I don't know how and where, but let's go somewhere." I replied, a surge of determination in my voice.

"Oh, an adventurous trip. I like it," she said, her eyes lighting up with excitement as she quickly got up.

Sometimes going without a plan is the best plan, I thought.

"Umm yeah. Every trip of ours is adventurous," I said.

She seemed to get a burst of energy, getting ready as quickly as she could. I also got up and dressed. Our bags were already packed from the previous day, so we were ready to go within 25 minutes. We skipped breakfast as the train was on time, and the station was only five minutes away—ten minutes if we didn't find a ride. We didn't want to take any risks this time.

We did a last-minute check of the lights and locked the door. Her excitement was on another level, and it felt good to see her that way. However, my mind was racing with too many calculations.

We planned to catch a train from Umaria to Katni, and from there, we hoped to head to Varanasi, although we weren't sure how. Interestingly, the train from Umaria was directly going to Varanasi. We could stay on the train and somehow work with the TC (Ticket Checker) to get us a berth. At that time, this was our best option.

We waited for an auto, but luck wasn't on our side, so we decided to walk. She was happily ready for it. I guessed she would have ridden a horse that day to get out of the village.

As we reached the station, we saw the display for the train coaches. On the IRCTC app, we found some unoccupied seats, a few of which were till Katni.

"S3, 43, 54, and a couple more are showing as unoccupied here," she said, looking at her phone. She was always quick at checking things.

"Okay, great. We'll get into S3 and hope it's not occupied," I said.

The train slowed in front of us as we waited for the S3 coach.

"It's too crowded; those seats will definitely be occupied," she said, her enthusiasm wavering.

"We'll manage. Just don't say anything and nod at whatever I say," I instructed.

"Hmm," she murmured in agreement.

As the train stopped, we made our way through the crowd, carefully squeezing past luggage and people. As expected, some people were sleeping. A boy in his 20s, wearing a torn shirt and covered in paint, was lying on seat 41. Nearby, a woman and some kids were sitting in seats 38 and 42. I was pretty sure those seats weren't theirs, so I decided to try my luck with the boy.

"Hey! This seat belongs to us," I said firmly, hoping to sound authoritative.

The boy was half asleep or maybe just didn't want to respond. I tried again, this time with more persistence, "Hey! Get up, this seat is ours."

This time he looked at us, groggy and slightly irritated. "This is ours, 41 and 42," I said, pointing at the seats with determination.

He didn't argue and began to get up, though slowly, making it clear he wasn't happy about it. Eventually, he stepped down, and we decided to share the same seat since it was only a 1-2 hour journey to Katni.

"You lie down," I said to Purvi, giving her a reassuring smile and patting the seat.

"Nah, I'm fine. But what's next?" she asked, her eyebrows furrowed with concern, echoing the question already swirling in my mind.

I started after a pause, taking a deep breath. "See, we can take a car from Katni to Varanasi, but that will be costly," I said, looking into my phone as I navigated the Ola/Uber apps. "Or this train will also go to Varanasi directly, but it's a long journey, and we don't even have a proper seat or food. Also, if the TC comes, we may have to bear a fine. Also, I'm hungry," I added, my stomach growling in agreement.

In all the rush, we forgot to pack any snacks and hadn't had breakfast either and it was already 11 AM.

"Me too," she responded, nodding in agreement, her eyes reflecting the same hunger.

"Let's get down at Katni then?" she suggested, her voice hopeful and eyes slightly brightening.

"Yes, I think so. That will be better. We will have some food first. We can go to Pizza Hut," I said, my mouth watering at the thought of pizza.

"Pizza! Yes! Also, there are a few bus options available as well," she said, showing her phone with a gleam in her eye.

"Okay, yes, we can consider it. Also, we can try some local cabs," I said, feeling a bit more optimistic as I saw some feasible options.

"So, we are getting down at Katni?" she asked for confirmation, her eyes searching mine for assurance.

"Umm, yeah, let's do that. First eat and then we'll see," I said, unable to control my hunger, my mind set on pizza.

"Also, before that, we need to confirm with the hotel if our bookings are still valid and available,"

I said, my voice filled with concern. It was the Dev Deepawali Festival in Varanasi, a grand event with huge crowds gathering every year. So, even if someone had bookings, there was a high chance they might get altered.

"Hmm," she responded, her worried look reflecting my own concerns.

Time was passing very slowly, and it felt like ages before we reached Katni. The train kept making multiple unplanned stops. With each stop and each passing moment, we kept rethinking our decision, continuously checking options on our phones.

Finally, the train started slowing down as Katni station approached. We got up from our seat, checked for any left belongings, and moved towards the train's gates. We finally reached Katni by 12PM. My mind was racing with thoughts about how we would travel, whether our hotel booking was still valid, what if it wasn't, should we have stayed on the train to Varanasi, and whether we should even go to Varanasi or try another place. But amid all these thoughts, the top priority was deciding what kind of pizza I would eat. Pizza beats all.

We headed straight to Pizza Hut after getting down at Katni, which was only a two-minute walk from the station. Our eyes were split between the road and our phones, searching for ways to reach Varanasi. We reached Pizza Hut and grabbed a corner seat. It wasn't crowded, just 1-2 groups, as expected on a Saturday afternoon. We placed our bags at our table, and I went to the counter to order our usual choice.

"Uhh, one Peppy Paneer and one Farmhouse," I said to the lady at the counter, my anticipation growing with each passing second.

"Regular size, sir?" she asked while entering the details into her machine.

"Yes," I replied, trying to hide my impatience but failing.

"That'll be 520 rupees, sir. Cash or online?" she asked, her eyes meeting mine briefly.

"Online," I said, taking out my phone to scan the QR code, my fingers trembling slightly from hunger and excitement.

After making the payment and collecting the receipt, I returned to our seat. Our order should be ready in 10 minutes, she said.

"It's 4000 bucks for the bus journey," Purvi said as soon as I sat down, her voice tinged with disbelief and worry.

"What? 4000 for two people is too costly, that too for a bus journey," I replied, my eyebrows shooting up in surprise.

"4000 for a single person," she said, her face showing a mix of frustration and disbelief.

"What!!" I exclaimed, my eyes widening in shock.

"Hmm," she said, showing her phone with a resigned expression.

"Let me check some local cab options," I said, feeling the weight of disappointment settling in. I did some Google searches and made a few calls for local cabs to Varanasi, but they were either too expensive or unavailable.

I had almost lost all hope of getting to Varanasi and was very hungry when our pizza call came. I quickly grabbed our pizzas. The paneer, capsicum, and tomato toppings on one, and mushrooms and jalapenos on the other, looked delicious. We quickly spread the chili flakes and oregano, took out the ketchup, and took the first slice. It was heavenly.

After finishing the pizza and regaining some strength, we decided to gather our hopes again. We first thought of checking with our hotel. I made a call to OYO, and after multiple tries, they connected me to the hotel reception. As expected, they denied providing the room at the previous tariff and asked for an additional 500 bucks. After some arguing, I finally gave up and agreed to the increased tariff, but even then, he didn't guarantee the room.

"But our train is late, and we'll be reaching late at night. So, we can get the room then, right?" I asked, trying to confirm, a hint of desperation in my voice.

"By what time will you arrive?" the hotel guy asked, his tone slightly impatient.

"Can't say as of now, but it could be around 11 PM-12 AM based on the current train situation," I said, my voice reflecting the uncertainty and worry.

"Ohh, that's too late. Ahh…Bhaiya, you can check once you arrive, but I can't guarantee you a room as there are too many people already in line, and if you don't come, we will be at a loss," he said, his tone apologetic but firm.

He wasn't wrong, and I understood his concern. I asked for his number to avoid the hassle of going through OYO again.

"Ahh...ok...it's बहत्तर, चार सौ अस्सी, सात सौ सड़सठ, अट्ठानबे," he started dictating in Hindi. I quickly turned to Purvi to help me with the English translation and relayed it to her.

"72, 480, 767, 89," she typed into her phone, her fingers moving quickly.

But our hopes were dashed again after this call. Not only were we unsure about how to get there, but now we didn't even have a confirmed place to stay. I looked at Purvi, and she understood my tension.

"Let's go to Jabalpur instead," she suggested, her voice filled with resolve. Jabalpur was only a 3-4 hour journey from Katni, and many local trains ran that way, making it an easier commute. I checked for trains, and there was a local at 2 pm, just 20 minutes from now.

I nodded, and we made our way back to the station. I could sense her disappointment as she really wanted to go to Varanasi for Dev Deepawali.

"We can still go to Varanasi. We might find some seats and can talk to the TC and try our luck. Also, let me check with the hotel if they can confirm the room if we deposit something," I said, trying to lift her spirits and asked for her phone to dial the number she had stored.

The number you are trying to call doesn't exist. *Jis number se aap sampark karna chahte hai wo upyog me nahi hai.*

My face fell, and I felt a deep sense of frustration. I handed over the phone to her. She was also shocked, her eyes widening in disbelief.

"See, we tried everything. Maybe we weren't destined to go to Varanasi. Please don't be upset," I said, trying to console her, my voice soft and reassuring, placing a comforting hand on her shoulder.

She nodded, her eyes glistening with unshed tears, a small smile trying to form on her lips.

"Let's go to Jabalpur. We have a local train in 10 minutes, and I promise we will have great fun. We will eat, go to the movies, and do some shopping," I continued, my voice filled with determination to make the best of the situation.

"Hmm, okay," she said, her voice tinged with reluctant acceptance.

We reached the station, and I went to the ticket counter and bought two general tickets for Jabalpur for 60 bucks. The local train was already stationed at Platform 1. We quickly went inside and searched for vacant seats. It didn't take much effort, and we found seats. We put our bags above and finally settled. I took my earphones and plugged in some calm music to take a quick nap. Purvi got busy on her mobile, looking up a Jabalpur itinerary.

The train departed on time. Lost in my thoughts, I reflected on what a day it had been.

"AMAN!!" shouted Purvi, her voice filled with alarm, hearing the announcement in the train.

"Iss train me apka swagat hai. Ye Katni se Satna tak jayegi." (Welcome to this train. It will be going from Katni to Satna.)

We had gotten on the wrong train. Our train to Jabalpur was also a local train from Katni at 2 pm but from Platform 6. This train was going in the opposite direction to Jabalpur, to Satna, which is on the way to VARANASI.

We were in total shock. What had just happened? How could this be possible? We checked our phones again, hoping for clarity. There were two trains scheduled at the same time, and in our haste, we had boarded the wrong one—or had we actually made the right choice after all?

Purvi and I looked at each other, utterly clueless. "Should we get down at the next station and catch a train to Jabalpur from there?" I suggested, trying to come up with a solution.

"The next station is 'Patwara,' a very small stop where hardly any trains make a halt," she replied, her voice tinged with concern. "After that, we have 'Maihar' station."

"But going back to Jabalpur from Maihar doesn't seem worth the effort," I mused. "What if we go to Varanasi instead?"

"Varanasi?!" she exclaimed, her eyes lighting up with excitement.

"Yes, maybe it's fate. Maybe God wants us to be in Varanasi after all," I said, smiling at the thought.

"Okay, but..." she trailed off, uncertainty creeping into her voice.

"See, this train goes to Satna. From Satna, we can catch many direct trains to Varanasi. Let me check," I said, pulling out my phone to look up the schedules.

"Wait, I'll check too," she said, quickly opening her phone.

We both got absorbed in our searches, exploring all possible routes and combinations. It turned out that we had a good chance of getting to Varanasi. We just needed to switch trains at Satna, and we could be in Varanasi before midnight.

"There are two trains from Satna around 5 PM. They both reach Varanasi around midnight, and this train will get us to Satna by 4 PM," I explained, feeling more optimistic.

"Yes, that's right! Let's go to Varanasi, finally!!" I said, excitement bubbling up.

"Yippee! But wait," she said, her expression shifting from joy to worry.

"What about our stay?" she asked, a genuine concern in her eyes.

I had been thinking about that too. "I'm not going to lie to you," I began, pausing to gather my thoughts.

She looked at me intently, waiting for the rest of my response. "There might be a chance that we'll have to spend the entire night at the ghats. Arriving around midnight during the festival season, finding a room could be quite difficult," I said, trying to prepare her for the possibility.

Her face showed signs of worry, but I quickly continued. "But I have some addresses and contacts for hotels near *Assi Ghat*. We'll go to each one and try to find a room," I said, hoping to reassure her.

She took a deep breath and nodded. "Okay, let's do it. Varanasi, here we come!"

We settled back into our seats, the initial shock giving way to a new sense of adventure. The thought of wandering the ancient streets of Varanasi under the night sky, exploring the ghats, and experiencing the vibrant festival atmosphere filled us with excitement. This unexpected detour might just turn out to be the best part of our journey.

Our thoughts were interrupted as the train made a stop at Maihar. The next station was Satna. The excitement between us was palpable; neither of us had anticipated these turns of events.

"I'm so excited," she said, her eyes sparkling.

"Are you? Are you also excited?" she continued, nudging my shoulder playfully.

I nodded, lost in thought. My mind was racing with all the scenarios that could unfold in Varanasi. What if we didn't get a room? Where would we go in Varanasi at midnight? All these thoughts swirled around, clouding my excitement.

"Come on, don't be such a bore," she chided gently. "You were in such a bad mood since November 19th, but at least now be happy. We are going to Varanasi!"

"Uff! Not that, not November 19th," I groaned inwardly. She had touched a raw nerve. November 19, 2023, was a nightmare for every Indian cricket fan. It was the night of the ODI World Cup Final 2023. India had performed exceptionally well throughout the tournament, winning all the matches, but then came the final against Australia. We were all so excited, so hyped, as India had not won the cup since 2011. "Dhoni finishes off in style. A magnificent strike into the crowd! India lifts the World Cup after

28 years!" Those words from Ravi Shastri still ring in the ears of every Indian during every cricket tournament.

We had all gathered in Indore, confident that India would win. We made plans for celebrations after the match. But we lost. We lost badly, and I was still not over it. She had inadvertently dragged me back to those painful memories, that nightmare, that night.

I looked at her, trying to control my anger. "I AM HAPPY, OK?" I said, my voice strained.

She understood and stayed calm. "Okay, okay," she said softly.

We realized that the train had been at Maihar station for the past hour, and some passengers were even exiting and boarding other trains. We checked our phones.

"If this train stays here for another 30 minutes, there's a chance we'll miss the train from Satna," I said, worry creeping into my voice.

"Should we board that train?" she asked, pointing to a train at platform 1 heading to Satna. Ours was on platform 2, so to board it, we would have to cross the rail tracks and get inside the other train. Taking the stairs would take more time, and the train might depart by then. Other people were following the same approach, getting off our train on the railway tracks and boarding the other one.

"Uh, I don't know," I said, hesitant. I was thinking that what if our local train departed first? We still had 30 minutes, so should we wait? Plus, the other train looked too crowded.

The siren wailed, but it was for the other train, and it left while we were still thinking.

Another 15 minutes passed, and our train still hadn't moved. To our surprise, one more train arrived.

Without wasting much time, we decided to board it, but via the railway track route as the stoppage was for only 2 minutes.

We quickly grabbed our bags and ran on the railway tracks to platform 1, reaching the gate of the new train. It was extremely crowded, with people standing at the gates, leaving not much space for us to get in. I was rethinking my decision, but we had no other choice. Somehow, we managed.

I got on first, as it's difficult to climb into the train with our bags.

"Give me the bag. Come on, quick," I said after getting into the train.

She handed me the bag. I placed it on the side of the gate and took her hand to help her climb up.

We did it. We were finally in the train. The sense of accomplishment was palpable as we navigated through the crowded compartment, trying to find a place for her to sit. The train was packed, with people standing in the aisles, bags and belongings cluttering every available space. After navigating through a few seats, we found a small spot at the edge of a seat. I signalled her to sit and placed our bags down.

"Sit here," I said, guiding her into the small space.

She smiled gratefully as she sat down, and I took a deep breath, feeling a wave of relief wash over me. We had caught this train against all odds, and if everything went smoothly, we would reach Satna on time for our next connection.

The train jerked forward as it departed the station, the rhythmic clatter of wheels on tracks blending with the chatter of passengers. There was a family seated in front of us, likely coming from Kolkata, and they were in the midst of a meal, their parathas emitting a tempting aroma that filled the compartment. The smell reminded me that we hadn't eaten yet, and we needed to order food or we'd go hungry on our journey.

"Please, have some," the kind lady from the family said, offering a paratha to Purvi.

"Nah, thanks, I'm good," Purvi replied, politely declining the offer.

I couldn't help but wonder why they hadn't offered me any food. Ignoring my brief moment of pique, I quickly opened the Swiggy app and entered our location as Satna Station. I scrolled through the food options and showed them to Purvi for her confirmation.

"I'm ordering food at Satna. Khichdi for myself. What will you have?" I asked.

"Umm, same," she said after a moment's thought.

"Okay. Anything else?" I inquired.

"Umm... no," she replied, but then quickly added, "Wait! Is chai or coffee available? I could really go for a kadak chai or coffee right now."

I searched for hot beverage options. "Yes, added and ordered," I said, confirming the order with a sense of satisfaction.

The train was running at a good pace, and we were on track to reach Satna on time. I glanced at Purvi, who seemed lost in thought, her eyes tracing the patterns of the passing scenery. I wondered what was going through her mind— whether she was as worried about the next steps as I was, or if she was simply enjoying the moment.

As we approached Satna, the train began to slow down, the brakes squealing in protest. The station came into view, a bustling hub of activity. Vendors were selling snacks and tea, porters were rushing about, and passengers were milling around, either waiting to board or disembark.

"We're almost there," I said, nudging Purvi gently.

She straightened up, a look of determination replacing her earlier introspection. "Let's get ready. We don't have much time between trains."

We gathered our bags and made our way towards the door, joining the throng of passengers preparing to get off. The train came to a halt, and we stepped onto the platform, immediately enveloped by the chaotic energy of the station.

We both needed to use the restroom, so we quickly moved to the waiting area. The delivery guy was showing 20 minutes for the khichdi and

25 minutes for the chai, and our train was scheduled to arrive in 25 minutes as well. We were really running against the clock. After using the restroom, I handed our bags to Purvi.

"You wait here. I'll go collect our food at the entrance. The chai guy hasn't reached the restaurant yet, and I'm not sure he'll be able to make it. But the khichdi should be here any minute. Let me grab that," I said.

"Okay, if it takes too long, just cancel the order for chai," she replied.

"Alright, I will," I said and hurriedly made my way to the main entrance to collect our khichdi. I was constantly tracking and calling the delivery guy to get updates on our order, but he was stuck in traffic. Frustrated, I had no other option but to cancel the chai order, even though it still charged me the whole amount.

I finally collected the khichdi order and returned to Purvi. We considered eating in the waiting area, but we didn't have time, and she wasn't feeling hungry.

"Should we eat?" I suggested.

"We'll eat on the train. I'm not feeling hungry right now," she said.

"Alright," I replied, and we hoisted our bags onto our shoulders and headed to Platform 4. There were two trains to Varanasi from Satna. One was the current train and the other an express arriving 10 minutes later. We decided to go with the first train, hoping it would get us there earlier.

When we arrived at Platform 4, the train numbers and coaches were displayed, but to our surprise, there were no sleeper, AC, or other reserved coaches—only general compartments. It was quite a surprise for such a long-route train to have only general coaches.

"All general coaches!" I exclaimed.

"Maybe it's a passenger train, that's why," I continued.

"It's quite a long-distance train. I'm surprised it's all general," she said, looking at her phone.

"Should we go or not?" she asked.

"Ah, let's see if it's not overcrowded, we'll go," I said, waiting for the train to arrive.

As the train approached and slowed down, our expressions changed from uncertainty to cautious optimism. We couldn't decide whether to be happy or worried because the train wasn't overcrowded—in fact, it was almost empty. There were hardly four or five people sitting in each coach, which generally accommodates hundreds of passengers.

We both hesitated, unsure whether to board the train. But seeing some people getting in gave us some courage. I looked at Purvi and nodded yes. As I stepped into the train, I looked up and silently prayed for a safe journey.

"What an irony," I muttered. "Normally, people look for less crowded coaches in a train to settle in, but here we are searching for a coach with some crowd."

After going through two or three coaches, we saw a middle-aged man sitting with two kids, with empty seats in front of him. There were a few more people in the coach, which made it feel safe.

"Shall we sit here?" I murmured.

"Yes," she nodded.

We finally got settled and relaxed. The empty seats allowed us to stretch our legs and sit comfortably. The train was running faster than we expected, which was a relief. We checked the status of the other train, and it was pretty much behind us. This made us think we had made the right choice.

But soon, our happiness was disrupted as the train took an unexpected halt in the middle of nowhere.

"AMAN!" Purvi exclaimed.

"I can't find this train anywhere on the official IRCTC app," she continued, her voice filled with worry.

"What!? How is that possible?" I said, quickly checking my phone.

Sure enough, there was no train listed with that number on the official app. We could only see it on an unofficial tracking app. We were totally clueless.

"We will reach Varanasi, right?" she asked, worry evident in her voice.

"Yes, yes. There may be some error on IRCTC, but the tracking app shows Varanasi, right? We will, of course," I said, trying to reassure her.

To add to our fear, the coach lights started flickering, and it was only happening in our coach. All the other coach lights were working properly.

"What is happening?" she said, her voice trembling.

"It's only happening in this coach. Shall we move to a different coach?" I asked, equally unnerved.

Suddenly, the lights got fixed. "Let's stay here. Other people are also here," she said, trying to calm down.

We decided to have our dinner. The khichdi tasted good, or maybe we were just very hungry.

Throughout the rest of the journey, the train took many halts, and both our train and the other express train were running one after the other. The express train had covered the distance and was now running just behind us. We kept tracking the train, reassuring ourselves that we would reach Varanasi.

After a journey full of surprises, adventure, shock, fear, and halts, we were finally nearing Varanasi. As the train slowed down, we both looked at each other and shared a smile of relief and excitement.

"Finally, we reached Varanasi," I said, feeling a mixture of exhaustion and exhilaration.

Stepping off the train, the cool night air of Varanasi greeted us, filled with the distant sounds of the bustling city. The station was alive with activity despite the late hour, a stark contrast to our eerily quiet train ride.

When I put my hands in my pocket because it was a little cold, I felt something. It was two tickets to Jabalpur. Seeing them, a smile spread across my face, and I thought, 'It's like God is watching over us, saying, you wanted an adventurous trip!' *When he decides to play the game...then he is the only player and also... the only spectator.*

Plan all you want, prepare all you can...but in the end...destiny unfolds only as He (God) desires.

We think we can decide our future with plans and predictions, but we often forget that, we are merely puppets in God's universe. And to be here, in Kashi—the oldest city where Mahadev himself resides—you truly need his blessing and permission.

"We made it," Purvi said, her eyes shining with excitement.

It was 2 AM, and the station was almost empty, as expected. A cold breeze filled the air, carrying a different sense of religious belief that runs deep in the heart of Kashi. The atmosphere was a pure bliss, and it felt like all our tiredness had vanished.

As we stepped out of the station, the quietude of the night was occasionally broken by the soft murmur of distant temple bells and the chanting of prayers. The city seemed to be whispering its ancient secrets to us. The lights from the ghats and temples reflected on the serene waters of the Ganges, creating a mystical aura.

"Can you feel it?" Purvi asked, her voice filled with awe. "There's something magical about this place."

"Yes, you feel a sense of calmness even with so much chaos around.," I replied, taking in the sights and sounds.

Soon a cluster of autos and rickshaws gathered around, their drivers eagerly asking about our destination.

"Assi Ghat. How much?" I asked one of the auto drivers.

"300 bucks," the autowala replied without hesitation.

"What? That's too much. It's hardly 6 kilometers," I protested.

"It's midnight, sir. Rates are higher now because we won't get any return fare," he explained.

I moved on to a cycle rickshaw, thinking it would be cheaper, though slower. An old man was paddling it, and despite my concerns about speed, I figured we had nowhere to rush. We climbed in, but I quickly realized my mistake. We were moving at a snail's pace, after nearly 30 minutes, we had only covered half the distance. But we didn't mind. In that moment, there was a magical peace—just us, moving slowly through the quiet streets, with no traffic or minimal people around. *Just like we play a video at slow-speed to understand better... life too... at times... needs a slow button—to breathe, to feel, to understand.*

We finally reached Assi Ghat, but the rickshaw driver refused to take us to the exact hotel location. I didn't argue much, unsure if it would even be our final stop or if we would need to search for more hotels. I had already searched for a few hotel options near Assi Ghat and stored their addresses on my phone.

We made our way towards the guesthouse we had booked, our footsteps echoing in the stillness of the night. The narrow lanes were deserted, but the walls were adorned with vibrant murals and posters of upcoming religious events. The air was thick with the scent of incense and marigolds, further enhancing the sacred ambiance.

We reached the location. However, the main door was locked. Despite knocking and ringing the bell multiple times, no one answered. I called the number displayed on the board, but there was no response.

"Let's go from here. Come on, let's go," Purvi said, clearly frustrated.

"Go? Where? Where will we go? Just wait, let me try again," I said, equally frustrated but trying to stay calm.

I called again, and thankfully, someone answered.

"Bhaiya, hello. We have a booking and we are standing outside your main gate," I said urgently.

"What? What booking, sir? By what name? Did you make any payment?" he asked, sounding half-asleep. "Also, no rooms are available at the moment."

"No, we didn't make a payment, but you said the booking was confirmed. Can you please help us? I'm with my wife, and we're standing outside. Can you please come once?" I pleaded.

"You came with a lady? What to do now, no rooms are available. Okay wait, I'm coming," he said.

After a couple of minutes, we heard someone coming from inside the hotel and unlocking the gate. He greeted us and welcomed us into the reception area.

"Sir, you are with a lady. I can't ask you to leave at this hour, but I can't arrange a room either since everything is booked until tomorrow," he said, looking more tense than us.

He discussed something with the reception guy and then turned back to us.

"Sir, I am arranging a room for you in a nearby hostel. Please manage for this night, and tomorrow we will see about getting you a room in this hotel. Don't worry, the bed and everything will be arranged in the hostel," he assured us.

We were more than okay with this and felt immensely grateful. He could have easily told us to leave, but he chose to help us, going out of his way. *Kindness doesn't cost a penny, yet it's still so rare.*

We followed the reception guy, who led us to the hostel and showed us the room.

"Thank you so much," I said, feeling a wave of relief wash over me.

"Yes, thank you," Purvi added, her voice filled with gratitude.

The hostel room was basic but clean. We settled in, finally able to rest after our long and unexpected journey. And in some hesitation purvi whispered to me, can I tell you something? But promise you won't get mad? I really don't have energy to get mad tell me.

I think I got the number wrong!, what number ? The hotels number which you dictated me when we were in Katni and then when you called that number it was not reachable,

Oh, that, I smiled, it was really our destiny to reach here.

The old city of Varanasi, with its charm and challenges, had already made an impression on us. As we lay down, exhausted but content, the distant sounds of temple bells and chants comforted us into a peaceful sleep, reminding us that we were in one of the most spiritual places in the world.

The next couple of days were a whirlwind of excitement, engagement, and pure awe. After the initial challenges of our unexpected journey, we found ourselves waking up in a modest but comfortable room at a small guesthouse near Assi Ghat. The room was cozy, with a wooden bed, a small wardrobe, and a window that offered a glimpse of the bustling streets below. The air was filled with a mix of incense and the faint aroma of street food, creating a sensory experience unique to Varanasi.

Our first full day in Varanasi began with the sound of temple bells and the distant chants of morning prayers. The city was already alive, a stark contrast to the quiet night we had arrived in. We decided to start our exploration at Assi Ghat, just a short walk from our guesthouse. As we stepped out, the narrow lanes were already crowded with locals and tourists alike, all moving with a sense of purpose and devotion.

From Assi Ghat, we made our way to Manikarnika Ghat, the most sacred and ancient ghat in Varanasi. Known as the "Burning Ghat," Manikarnika is where Hindus believe that cremation here leads to moksha, or liberation from the cycle of birth and death. The air was thick with smoke from the funeral pyres, and the atmosphere was sober yet profoundly spiritual. We stood in silence, witnessing the rituals of life and death unfold before us, a stark reminder of the transient nature of existence.

The following day, we decided to embark on a culinary adventure, eager to taste the flavours that Varanasi had to offer. Our first stop was the renowned *Kashi Chaat Bhandar*, a small but bustling eatery known for its delectable chaats. We ordered a plate of tamatar chaat, a tangy and spicy delight made with tomatoes, spices, and crispy sev. The explosion of flavours was unlike anything we had ever tasted, a perfect balance of sweet, sour, and spicy.

Next, we headed to *Deena Chat Bhandar*, another iconic chaat stall in Varanasi. We tried the famous aloo tikki, a potato patty served with chickpea curry, yogurt, and a medley of chutneys. We washed it down with a glass of lassi from the *Blue Lassi Shop*, a quaint little place known for its thick and creamy yogurt drinks. The lassi, flavoured with fresh fruits and nuts, was the perfect way to cool down after the spicy chaats.

Our culinary journey continued with a visit to *Ram Bhandar*, a legendary sweet shop in Varanasi. We indulged in a plate of *malaiyyo*, a frothy milk dessert topped with saffron and pistachios. The dessert was light and airy, melting in our mouths with a burst of creamy goodness.

The highlight of our trip was undoubtedly the Dev Deepawali festival, a celebration that transforms Varanasi into a city of lights. Held on the full moon night of the Hindu month of Kartik, Dev Deepawali is a grand spectacle where the ghats and the entire city are illuminated with millions of diyas (oil lamps). The festival marks the victory of Lord Shiva over the demon Tripurasur, and it is believed that the gods descend to Earth to bathe in the Ganges on this auspicious night.

As evening approached, we made our way to *Dashashwamedh Ghat*, the main ghat of Varanasi, known for its elaborate evening aarti (ritual of worship). The ghat was already crowded with devotees and tourists, all eagerly awaiting the start of the aarti. The air was filled with the sounds of conch shells, bells, and chants, creating an atmosphere of divine energy.

The aarti began with the lighting of the diyas, and soon the entire ghat was bathed in a warm, golden glow. Priests dressed in traditional attire performed the ritual with synchronized movements, waving large lamps and chanting hymns in praise of the Ganges. The sight was mesmerizing, a spiritual performance that captivated everyone present. As the aarti concluded, the sky lit up with a spectacular display of fireworks, each burst adding to the magic of the night.

We spent the rest of the evening wandering along the ghats, taking in the breathtaking sight of thousands of diyas floating on the river. The steps of each ghat were decorated with colourful rangolis (intricate patterns made with coloured powders), and the air was filled with the fragrance of incense and flowers. We joined the locals in releasing our own diyas into the Ganges, a symbolic gesture of offering and devotion.

As we made our way back to the guesthouse, we reflected on the incredible journey we had experienced over the past few days. Varanasi, with its rich history, spiritual significance, and vibrant culture, had left an indelible mark on our hearts. The Dev Deepawali festival, in particular, was a highlight that we would cherish forever. The sight of the city illuminated with millions of diyas, the sounds of the aarti, and the sense of devotion and unity among the people were truly unforgettable.

Despite the physical exhaustion from walking over 21 kilometers in three days, every step had been worth it. We had immersed ourselves in the essence of Varanasi, experiencing its spirituality, its chaos, and its beauty. As we packed our bags and prepared to leave, we felt a deep sense of gratitude for the experiences and memories we had gained.

After an unexpected and adventurous trip, we finally returned to Umaria and slipped back into our old routine. The train journey had given us time to reflect on the whirlwind of experiences in Varanasi, and as we arrived in the familiar surroundings of Umaria, it felt both comforting and anticlimactic.

We reached Umaria in the morning. Purvi, ever the dedicated professional, left for her bank job soon after we arrived. I opened my laptop and checked my emails, gradually easing myself back into work mode. The mundane tasks of the day provided a strange sense of normalcy after our recent excitement.

By noon, I realized I hadn't eaten anything substantial and decided to order lunch from our local restaurant. As usual, I got lost in my work, and before I knew it, it was 5 PM—time for Purvi to leave work. Our routine had always involved me meeting her halfway, and today was no different.

I picked up my phone and called her. "Hey, are you ready to leave?"

"Yes, just leaving in five minutes," she replied, her voice steady but with a hint of something unspoken.

"Okay, I'll meet you at our usual spot," I said, preparing to hang up.

There was a brief pause on the line. "Aman, wait..."

"Yeah? What is it?" I asked, sensing something was off.

"I missed my periods," she murmured, her voice barely audible.

"What? That means... I mean, you could be... we could be..." I stammered, my heart racing.

"Yes," she confirmed softly.

I was stunned. "But if you are... then... we did so many things that should be avoided in such condition and after Manali incident we promised to be more careful... we walked miles, ran on tracks, jumped into trains and what not. How could this happen?"

There was a moment of silence on the line, heavy with unspoken thoughts and emotions. "Can you pick up a pregnancy test on my way. Please leave quickly."

A thousand thoughts flooded my mind, some hopeful and others filled with anxiety. I quickly stopped by the local medical shop and asked for a pregnancy kit, my hands trembling slightly as I did.

When I met Purvi at our usual spot, we exchanged a look filled with a mixture of excitement, fear, and uncertainty. We walked home in silence, both lost in our thoughts. Once inside, Purvi immediately took the test.

We sat in complete silence, our eyes glued to the test as it slowly began to reveal its result. It was blurry—neither positive nor negative. Time seemed to stop, and the tension in the room grew heavier with each passing second. Our hearts pounded in our chests, our breath shallow and uneven. We couldn't look away, trapped in that one moment, torn between hope and fear. *Every second felt like it might break us, and yet we couldn't move.*

SECOND MONTH

The Unexpected Reaction

Getting the blurred result on the pregnancy test left us more anxious and worried than before. We couldn't make any decisions without knowing for sure. *It felt like the universe had pressed pause–blurry lines, blurry thoughts, blurry answers.*

"I'll take it again tomorrow morning," Purvi suggested, her voice laced with both hope and apprehension. "I have read that morning tests gives more accurate results."

"Hmm," I nodded, still lost in my own whirlwind of thoughts.

"But we don't have any more test kits, do we?" I asked, realizing our immediate need.

"Oh, right," she said, her eyes widening.

"I'll buy some more," I said, already moving toward the door in a hurry.

""Wait!" she called out, stopping me in my tracks.

"What now? I'm not waiting until tomorrow to get it," I said, frustration creeping into my voice.

"Your mobile," she said, holding up my phone.

"Oh," I grabbed it from her and hurried out.

On my way to the medical shop, a flood of thoughts ran through my mind. If we are pregnant, we will need to go back to our hometown. But how? We'll manage something with a tatkal ticket. If it's a boy, I will name him... And if it's a girl, I will call her... And what if it's twins? Wow, it could be twins! But what if we aren't pregnant? What if we face complications like last time? No, I won't let that happen.

I reached the medical store and saw another customer there, so I waited for a couple of minutes, feeling the seconds stretch like hours. Finally, it was my turn.

"Ahh, pregnancy test," I said quietly to the pharmacist.

He took out one kit, but I hesitated. "Give me three," I said, thinking it was better to have more, just in case.

I quickly made my way back home, eager to be with Purvi. I knew she must be dealing with a torrent of thoughts, just like I was.

She was waiting by the door and immediately opened it as I reached.

"Here, I got three just in case," I said, handing over the test kits.

"Should we set an alarm for tomorrow morning so you don't forget to take the test?" I suggested, trying to be practical.

"Don't worry, I won't. I can't," she said, her eyes reflecting a mix of determination and worry.

That night, there wasn't much to discuss. We had dinner in near silence and then tried to sleep, though sleep was elusive.

The next morning, I woke up early—around 6 AM..., and turned to wake Purvi. To my surprise, she was already up.

I looked around for her and found her sitting in a chair, using her phone, probably trying to find some answers.

"Hey, did you take the test?" I asked, my heart pounding.

"Yes," she said before I could finish my question.

"And?" I asked, my voice barely a whisper.

She showed me the test kit. For a moment, I felt as nervous as if awaiting the results of a crucial exam. The kit showed one pink line and the other blurred, just like before. Two pink lines indicate a positive result, and one pink line indicates negative. But for us, it was still unclear.

"What now?" I asked, my voice filled with frustration and confusion.

"I don't know," she replied, looking just as lost as I felt.

I thought for a moment, trying to come up with a solution. "Can we check with Pragati didi? She's a gynaecologist from your hometown, right? Plus, she knows you well. She'll give us the right advice," I suggested, hoping for some clarity.

"Ahh, I don't know," Purvi said, clearly hesitant.

"We don't have any other choice. I don't want to take any chances. Please, stop being shy and make the call," I urged, my anxiety getting the better of me.

After a moment of hesitation, she sighed, "Fine, I'll call her on my way to the office."

"Sure?" I asked, needing to confirm her decision.

"Yes, baba, surely," she said, trying to reassure me.

"Hmm," I replied, feeling a bit relieved.

As usual, she prepared food for me before leaving for the office. I was left alone, anxiously waiting for her call. Every minute felt like an eternity. Finally, my phone rang. It was her.

"Ha, tell me, what did she say? Tell me fast," I said, unable to contain my eagerness.

"I asked her about the blurred line. She said it can be anything, either positive or negative, and advised me to wait for 3-4 days to recheck," Purvi explained.

"What?! That's all she said? Even we knew that already. That's why we needed confirmation!" I said, frustration bubbling over.

"Hmm," she said quietly, not adding anything more.

I hung up, feeling a wave of frustration wash over me. That day, I couldn't eat or work properly. All I could think about was whether we were pregnant and the need to consult a doctor immediately if we were. The uncertainty was driving me crazy.

I decided we needed to visit a clinic and get a proper test done, even though Umaria didn't have the best medical facilities. I wanted to leave for Burhanpur as soon as we knew for sure, but until then, I had no choice but to visit any local facility that could provide some level of confirmation.

I called Purvi again. "How much longer will you be at work?" I asked.

"Umm, 10-15 minutes more. Why? What happened?" she asked, sensing my urgency.

"Nothing, I'll come to pick you up from the bank," I said.

"Okay, but leave in 5-10 minutes, not right now" she advised.

"Ok," I replied, but I couldn't wait and left immediately.

On my way, I did some quick Google searches and found a few pathology labs nearby that offered pregnancy tests. I made a note of their locations, determined to visit one right after picking up Purvi.

When I reached the bank, Purvi was already waiting outside, looking a bit more composed than I felt. we walk in silence for a while.

"Let's go to one of those pathology labs I found," I said, breaking the silence.

"Okay," she agreed, her voice steady.

We went to 'Rakesh Pathology', a small, modest establishment tucked away in a narrow street. The room was divided into two even smaller sections by a thin partition. One side served as the reception and waiting area, while the other was designated for tests and housed the necessary equipment.

"Uh, excuse me," I called out to a man working in the testing area.

"Yes?" he responded, looking up from his work.

"Is pregnancy testing done here?" I asked, feeling a mix of hope and apprehension.

"Yes, please enter your name, mobile number, and address," he said, showing us a register.

I filled in the details. "Name of the doctor who prescribed the test?" he asked.

"No doctor, we are just doing it ourselves," I replied.

He wrote "Personal" in the register and handed Purvi a pregnancy test kit, the same kind we had used at home.

I felt a bit surprised and skeptical. "Is this the pregnancy test? But we already took this twice at home. I'm not sure what will change now," I thought, anxiously waiting for Purvi to come out.

Purvi went to the washroom with the kit. A few minutes later, she came out, leaving the kit inside for the examiner. He collected it and went to the investigation area.

I looked at her, silently asking about the result. "Same, one line is blurred," she replied, her voice tinged with disappointment.

I felt a wave of frustration. "How long will it take?" I asked the examiner.

"Two minutes," he said.

I was surprised and anxious. "Is this the pregnancy test? We could have done this at home for half the price. Is there any other procedure?" I asked.

"This is the only test," he said.

After two minutes, he came back with the results, carefully placing them in an envelope. I was on edge, desperate to see the result. "What is it?" I quickly grabbed the envelope from him and opened it.

POSITIVE.

The word stared back at me. It was positive. I felt a rush of excitement and disbelief. A huge smile spread across my face. I double-checked the name. It was Purvi Shroff.

"Is it really positive?" I asked the examiner, still in shock.

"Yes," he confirmed.

"But one line was blurred, right?" Purvi interjected, still uncertain.

"Yes, but it is positive. Sometimes the line appears blurred at the start of pregnancy," he explained.

WOW. We both were over the moon, still trying to digest the overwhelming moment. That small, unassuming shop had given us the most special moment of our lives, a memory we would forever cherish. *It was a powerful reminder that happiness doesn't require grand setups or luxurious things; it often comes in the simplest forms, unexpected and pure.* In that modest shop, we found a lifetime of memories.

We walked out of the pathology lab, feeling a lightness in our steps. The world around us felt full of promise.

"Can you believe it?" I asked, looking at Purvi, my heart swelling with joy.

"I know! It feels so surreal," she replied, her eyes sparkling with happiness.

"We need to tell our parents," I said, already imagining their reactions—joy, surprise, maybe even a few happy tears.

"Yes, but let's wait until we visit a proper doctor for confirmation," she suggested, always the voice of reason.

"You're right. Let's leave for home. I don't want to stay here and risk anything happening again," I said, my concern evident.

"Okay, but what about my work? How long are we going for?" she asked, a bit worried.

"I can't say exactly, but it might be for nine months," I replied, bracing for her reaction.

She looked surprised. "But I don't have that many leaves. What will I tell them?" she asked, her voice tinged with concern.

"For now, just say there's a family emergency. We can figure out the rest later," I suggested.

"But there are some important tasks I planned to complete tomorrow, some pending files," she continued, clearly conflicted.

"Look, let's go to your bank and finish whatever is absolutely crucial right now. If you can't, we'll have to leave it. Our first priority is a proper check-up. Everything else can wait," I said firmly, trying to ease her mind.

She nodded, agreeing reluctantly. We hailed an auto and headed to her bank. As she went inside to wrap up her work, I stayed outside, frantically searching for tickets to get us home.

I tried every site, every combination of trains, but couldn't find any available tickets for today or even tomorrow. My frustration grew, but I wasn't giving up.

I called my father, hoping he could help with booking agents. "Ha, papa, can you send me a booking agent's number now?" I asked urgently.

"Okay, for whom?" he asked, a bit puzzled.

"We're coming home," I said, trying to keep the conversation brief.

"Okay, I'll share it right away," he said.

"Please send it quickly, bye," I said and hung up.

Within seconds, a WhatsApp notification appeared with the agent's details. I immediately called him.

"Hello, Pintu bhaiya? I'm Aman, son of Sunil Shroff. I need two urgent tickets from Katni to Burhanpur, for today or tomorrow," I explained, desperation in my voice.

"Today? That's difficult, bhaiya. But I can try for tomorrow and get tickets from Jabalpur to Burhanpur, will that work?" he asked.

I thought for a moment. Jabalpur was the next station after Katni, and we had to go at any cost. "Yes, that will work," I said, relief washing over me.

"Okay, it's almost 7 PM now. I'll update you by 9 PM," he promised.

"Okay, thank you," I said, hanging up.

When Purvi came out of the bank, she looked relieved but still worried. "Did you manage to get the tickets?" she asked.

"Almost. We might have to go from Jabalpur, but we should know by 9 PM," I said.

She sighed, a mix of relief and exhaustion on her face. "Okay, let's hope for the best," she said.

"Don't worry, everything will be fine. We're in this together," I reassured her, taking her hand as we made our way home to pack.

Just then I got a call from mom. I knew dad must have already told her about our ticket hunt, and she definitely had some questions about our last-minute travel plans.

"Yes, Mummy," I said, picking up the call.

"I heard you're planning to come. Is everything alright? What's with the sudden plan?" she asked, concern evident in her voice.

"Yes, everything is fine. We're just coming to visit, but we couldn't find any tickets," I said, trying to control my excitement about the news we had to share and my disappointment at not finding tickets.

"I called an agent, and he'll update us by 9 PM. Let's see," I continued.

"Okay, travel safe and keep me updated." she said before hanging up.

We reached home, and the wait for 9 PM felt endless. Purvi got busy with packing, knowing we might need to leave by tomorrow. Packing was crucial; we didn't want to forget anything important or misplace anything. We also had to organize and secure the things we weren't taking with us.

Just then, my phone rang again. It was Mom.

"We forgot that Priya is also coming to Burhanpur, and her train will make a stop at Katni station. If you can manage, you can travel with her," she said.

"Oh yes, that's possible! How did that slip my mind? Okay, let me call her right now," I said, feeling a surge of relief. It was a perfect solution to our problem.

I immediately called Priya, but she didn't pick up. I tried again. And again. Still no answer. My anxiety began to mount. I called mom again.

"Where is Priya?" I asked, unable to hide my frustration.

"What's happened?" she asked.

"She's not picking up. I've tried like 50 times," I said, exasperated.

"Okay, calm down. Let me call her," she said.

After a couple of minutes, mom called back. "She's not picking up my calls either," she said.

"WHAT THE HELL is wrong with this girl? Now what will we do? We have to reach Katni before 12, which means leaving by 10 PM. It's already 8:20 PM. We still need to finish packing and book something to reach Katni," I said, feeling the pressure mounting.

"I have the numbers of a few of her friends. Let me call them," she said.

"WAIT!! I'm getting a call from her—PRIYA!" I exclaimed and quickly switched to her call.

"Why weren't you picking up?" I demanded.

"What's wrong with you people? Twenty-two calls? I was sleeping, and my phone was on silent," she said, clearly annoyed.

"What? But? Anyway, listen, we need to go to Burhanpur. We can't get any tickets, so can we come with you? We can board from Katni," I explained quickly.

"But, I'm with my friends. How will we manage?" she replied, sounding reluctant.

Before she could respond, I hung up. My frustration was through the roof. But then, a minute later, she called back.

"Is it urgent and important?" she asked.

"Yes, it's really urgent and important," I said, my voice reflecting the gravity of the situation.

"Okay, come. We'll manage," she said, finally agreeing.

Relief washed over me as I quickly gestured Purvi to start packing. We had just one hour to prepare for our departure to Katni, and the gravity of the situation hit us both. This might be our last time in this place, and we had to act swiftly and efficiently. The next hour was a whirlwind of activity, filled with urgency and a tinge of bittersweet nostalgia.

We didn't have the luxury of time to go through all our belongings meticulously. Instead, we threw open our suitcases and began tossing in everything we deemed essential. Day-to-day clothes, important files, laptops, accessories, medicines, and other crucial items went into the bags. We left behind utensils, furniture, most of our clothing, beds, books, and all other bathroom and food products. It was a stark reminder of how quickly our lives were about to change.

"Don't forget the important documents!" Purvi called out as she rummaged through a drawer.

"I've got them! Make sure you pack the medicines, accessories and stuff," I replied, my mind racing through a mental checklist.

The kitchen became a scene of organized chaos as we multitasked like never before. Purvi was chopping vegetables while I packed some of our things. Then, we switched roles—she cooked rice while I checked and packed more items. The air was thick with the aroma of cooking and the sound of zippers and the rustle of clothing being packed away.

"Can you believe we're doing this? I hope everything will be fine" Purvi asked, her voice a mix of disbelief and excitement.

"Yes, don't worry, it will be" I said, trying to reassure her and myself.

We managed to eat and pack within the tight timeframe, our nerves heightened with every passing minute. Amidst the flurry, I also booked a cab from Umaria to Katni. Thanks to Purvi's good contacts in the area, it didn't take much effort—just a single call, and the cab was arranged.

"Do we have everything?" I asked, scanning the room one last time.

"Yes, I think we do. Let's just hope we haven't missed anything important," Purvi replied, her eyes reflecting a mix of anxiety and determination.

The cab arrived on time, the driver calling for our exact location. I directed him to a nearby landmark, "Gupta Kirana," a spot known to us and significant in our daily routine. As we loaded our bags into the cab, a wave of nostalgia washed over us. We were about to leave Umaria, a place that had become a part of us, filled with wonderful people and countless unforgettable memories.

Our entire lives were about to change that night. As we settled into the cab, the reality of our departure began to sink in. The streets of Umaria, familiar and comforting, passed by in a blur through the windows. Each turn, each shop, each face we saw triggered a flashback, a flood of memories that underscored just how deeply we were attached to this place. The small grocery store where we shopped, the railway tracks where we spent lazy Sunday afternoons, the bustling market that always had the freshest produce—each spot held a special place in our hearts.

Purvi sat beside me, her hand tightly gripping mine. "It's really happening," she whispered, her voice tinged with both sadness and anticipation.

"Yes, it is," I replied, trying to put on a reassuring smile. "But we'll make new memories, wherever we go."

She nodded, though her eyes remained fixed on the passing scenery. "Do you think we'll ever come back here?" she asked, her voice almost drowned out by the hum of the cab.

"I don't know," I admitted. "But even if we don't, this place will always be a part of us."

The road stretched out before us, each mile taking us further from the life we knew and closer to an uncertain future. *The last goodbye is always the hardest, and the uncertainty made it even more difficult.*

There was a lump in my throat, a mix of excitement for what was to come and sorrow for what we were leaving behind.

As we drove past 'Kanha Restaurant', memories of countless dinners and deep conversations filled my mind. "Remember our first date here?" I said, pointing to the restaurant as it disappeared behind us.

Purvi smiled, a tear rolling down her cheek. "Of course. You didn't like the food at all"

"But later, I was the one who insisted we go there for dinners and always used to order the same palak paneer," I added, laughing softly at the memory.

The cab continued to wind through the streets, each landmark pulling at our heartstrings. The small temple where we sought solace, the railway station from where we caught countless trains, the little kirana store from where use to buy almost everything—all these places had woven themselves into the fabric of our lives.

As we neared the outskirts of Umaria, the lights of the town began to fade. The driver, sensing our mood, remained silent, giving us the space to process our emotions. The silence in the cab was thick with unspoken words and shared memories.

"Do you think they'll miss me?" Purvi whispered, almost to herself.

"Of course they will," I said "Just as much as we'll miss them."

The road ahead was long, and our journey had just begun. But as we left Umaria behind, we carried with us the love, the memories, and the experiences that had shaped us. Our hearts were heavy, but also filled with hope for the future.

We finally reached Katni station, our nerves tingling with a mix of exhaustion and anticipation. The driver stopped, and I handed over the cash, thanking him for the ride. He gave us a sympathetic nod, perhaps sensing the gravity of our situation. I gathered our luggage, taking care to carry the heavier suitcases myself. I didn't want Purvi to strain herself in her condition.

"Let's get inside," I said to Purvi, who looked around, trying to get her bearings in the bustling station.

As we moved towards the entrance, we learned that our train was delayed by two hours. Instead of arriving at midnight, it was now scheduled for 2 AM. We made our way to the waiting area, trying to find a spot to settle down.

"I'll go get General tickets for Burhanpur, just in case," I told Purvi. "Stay here and rest. We might not need them, but it'll be good to have something to show the TT if there's a check."

She nodded, settling onto a bench. I could see the weariness in her eyes, but she still managed a brave smile. "I'll be fine. Just hurry back."

The ticket counter was a short walk away, but the queue moved slowly. As I stood there, my mind raced with thoughts of what lay ahead. The uncertainty of the night, the upcoming journey, and the weight of our news pressed heavily on me. I finally got the tickets and returned to Purvi, who was resting with her eyes closed.

"Got them," I said, handing her a ticket. "How are you holding up?"

"I'm okay," she replied, though I could hear the fatigue in her voice. "It's just a couple more hours."

We checked the train status obsessively, our eyes glued to our phones. Then, we noticed another train to Burhanpur arriving in 20 minutes. "What do you think?" I asked. "Should we try to catch this one? It might be better than waiting around."

Purvi hesitated, then nodded. "Ok, let's check it out."

We gathered our belongings and hurried to platform 4. The train pulled in, and we were met with a familiar sight: packed compartments, people standing shoulder to shoulder. My heart sank. We'd travelled in such conditions before, but this time was different. I looked at Purvi, and the thought of her enduring a crowded, uncomfortable journey made me uneasy.

"We can't do this," I said, shaking my head. "It's too risky with your condition. We'll wait for Priya's train."

Purvi sighed but agreed. "You're right. It's better to be safe."

We returned to the waiting area, the minutes dragging on as we tried to find some bit of comfort on the hard benches. The station's fluorescent lights cast a harsh glow, and the constant announcements echoed in the background. It felt like time had slowed to a crawl.

Finally, around 2 AM, the announcement for Priya's train crackled through the speakers. We gathered our belongings once more and made our way to the designated platform.

As we hurried along the platform, we anxiously checked the coach display and made our way to B2, where Priya's seats were supposed to be. To our shock, both the gates to the B2 compartment were locked from the inside. Panic surged through me as I tried the doors again, banging and shouting, but no one responded. We had only a couple of minutes until the train departed.

I quickly dialled Priya's number, but she didn't answer. "Not again, Priya!" I muttered under my breath as I redialled. I could feel Purvi's anxiety rising beside me. Finally, after what felt like an eternity, Priya picked up the phone, her voice groggy with sleep.

"Priya, open the gate! We're outside and the train is about to leave!" I shouted into the phone.

Startled awake, Priya hurried to our rescue. The sound of her phone ringing and the persistent knocking on the gate also roused the ticket inspector (TT), who appeared half-asleep but alert enough to know something was amiss. Just as Priya unlocked the gate and we stepped inside, the TT approached us, suspicion evident in his eyes.

"Tickets, please," he demanded, clearly confident, we had none since no boarding was scheduled from this station.

I quickly helped Purvi inside, settling her down before turning to the TT. "Sir, please, let me explain," I began, trying to keep my voice calm and respectful. "We don't have confirmed tickets, but we have general tickets. My wife is pregnant, and we need to get home urgently. It's a family emergency."

The TT listened, his expression hardening. Priya and her colleagues chimed in, pleading with him to let us stay. "Sir, they can stay with us," Priya's friend offered. "We'll manage somehow."

The TT shook his head, unmoved. "I'm sorry, but rules are rules. You cannot stay without confirmed tickets." He turned to the police attendant, ordering him to escort us out.

Fury bubbled inside me as I saw Purvi, who had just settled in, being asked to leave. "Sir, you can't do this," I protested, trying to keep my voice steady. "I understand the rules, and I'm ready to pay the fine."

The TT paused, considering my words. After a moment, he nodded reluctantly. "Alright, pay the fine and you can stay."

I quickly handed over the money, feeling a mix of relief and frustration. Purvi got settled in Priya's seat while Priya and her friends adjusted themselves to make space for us. I found an empty spot on the floor, laid out a bedsheet, and tried to make myself as comfortable as possible.

But I couldn't sleep that night. Maybe it was because I was lying on the hard floor, or perhaps it was the uncertainty of what lay ahead. Thoughts raced through my mind: Will everything be fine? Are we really pregnant? These questions haunted me, making it impossible to rest. As I stared out the window, watching the dark scenery flash by, my mind seemed to run in sync with the rhythm of the train.

Each passing tree, each distant light flickering in the night, mirrored the swirl of emotions within me. Every time the train slowed or stopped, I snapped out of my thoughts, only to plunge back into them when it picked up speed again.

Purvi was sleeping, she was awakening occasionally, seeking reassurance even in her dreams. I knew she was going through the same whirlwind of emotions, though she was handling it with a calm I admired.

As the night dragged on, I watched the darkness gradually give way to the first light of dawn. The inky black sky began to lighten, turning shades of deep blue and then soft pink. It was a sight that brought a strange comfort, a reminder that no matter how long or dark the night, morning would always come.

The scenes outside the window started to change too. The empty fields and silent towns began to stir with the first signs of life. Farmers heading out to their fields, early risers preparing for the day. It was like watching a painting come to life, and in that moment, I felt a sense of peace.

As the train rumbled on, the passengers around us began to stir. People were waking up, stretching, and preparing for the day ahead. I noticed an empty seat and finally got a place to sit, positioning myself where I could keep an eye on Purvi. She was awake, but I urged her to stay rested. "We still have an hour to go," I reminded her gently.

Glancing over at Priya and her friends, I asked, "Did you guys manage to sleep okay? I hope we didn't cause too much trouble." They assured me they were fine, having adapted well to the crowded conditions. I felt a wave of gratitude and apologized for the inconvenience. Priya, always thoughtful, had already called Papa to bring snacks for her friends at the station, a gesture that warmed my heart.

I couldn't help but marvel at Priya's calmness. Despite our sudden plan and the obvious care I was taking of Purvi, she didn't ask any probing questions. If I were in her place, I'd be curious.

As we neared Burhanpur station, I turned to Priya and said, "We're almost there. Can you stay with Purvi while I get our luggage?" She nodded, her expression understanding and supportive.

The train began to slow, and the familiar sights of Burhanpur came into view. Memories of our life here flooded back, mingling with the anxiety and excitement of the present. I moved quickly through the compartment, gathering our bags and making sure we hadn't left anything behind. The anticipation of what lay ahead was palpable, a mix of nerves and hope.

Stepping off the train, the morning air was crisp and filled with the sounds of the bustling station. Papa was waiting on the platform, his face lighting up when he saw us. He waved, a big smile spreading across his face. "How was the journey?" he asked, taking some of the bags from me.

"It was... eventful," I replied, glancing at Purvi, who was now standing beside Priya.

Papa handed the snacks to Priya's friends, thanking them for their help. "You must be hungry. Let's get home and have a proper breakfast," he suggested, his tone warm and reassuring.

As we made our way out of the station, I felt a sense of relief mingled with the anticipation of what was to come. Burhanpur held the promise of answers, of family support, and of the beginning of a new chapter in our lives.

"Papa, why don't you go straight to the shop?" I suggested.

"Yes, it must be getting late for you," Purvi added.

"And since we're three people, we can't all fit on the bike comfortably," Priya pointed out.

"An auto would be the best option for us," I concluded.

"Alright, that makes sense. I'll head to the shop then," Papa agreed.

We got into the auto, the fare was pretty much fixed, and I wasn't in the mood to bargain. We loaded our bags and settled in. I turned to Purvi and suggested, "Why don't you call your mom and let her know we've arrived safely?"

Purvi nodded, pulling out her phone. "Good idea," she said. She dialled her mom's number and chatted for a few minutes, assuring her that we had reached Katni safely but deciding not to reveal anything about the pregnancy just yet.

I, on the other hand, was itching to tell Priya the news. I exchanged a glance with Purvi, and she nodded in agreement, giving me the go-ahead. I turned to Priya, my excitement barely contained. "Aren't you curious about why we made such a sudden plan? What was the urgency?" I asked.

Priya's eyes sparkled with mischief. "Bhabhi is pregnant, isn't she?" she said with a grin.

We both stared at her, taken aback. "How did you know?" Purvi asked, equally surprised.

"I mean, yes, we are still a bit unsure, but that's the reason," I confirmed. "But how did you possibly figure it out?"

Priya laughed, a twinkle in her eye. "I'm very intelligent, guys. And besides, the urgency, the way you were caring for Bhabhi and the amount of luggage you brought with you for a sudden trip, it all pointed to something big."

Purvi blushed a little, smiling. "Wow Di," she said.

Priya leaned in, her expression turning serious. "So, how are you feeling, Bhabhi? Any morning sickness yet?"

"Not really," Purvi replied, shaking her head. "Just a bit tired. We haven't even had a proper check-up yet, that's why we're heading home."

Priya nodded understandingly. "It makes sense. You should get checked as soon as possible."

As the auto bumped along the familiar roads, we couldn't help but let our minds drift to how our parents would react to the news. "How do you think our parents will react to this news?" I asked, glancing at Purvi.

I smiled softly. "Mummy has probably already guessed why we're coming. She always has a sixth sense about these things."

Priya nodded in agreement. "Yeah, Mummy will definitely know. She'll be over the moon. And Papa too. I can already imagine his reaction," Priya said with a giggle. "He'll probably be the first to start thinking for baby names."

"And Mummy will start knitting baby clothes immediately," I added, laughing.

Purvi's eyes twinkled with excitement. "And my Mom and Dad will be so happy too. My mom has been wanting this for so long. She always used to bug me about having a baby, saying, 'Just have the baby and we'll take care of the rest.' She's going to be ecstatic."

"I can already see her reaction," I added, chuckling. "Your mom will probably be jumping with joy. It's going to be a moment worth capturing and framing."

Purvi nodded, a dreamy look on her face. "Yes, I'm eagerly waiting for that moment. I can't wait to see their faces when we tell them. It's going to be a moment we'll never forget.

Priya leaned in, her curiosity piqued. "So, what's the plan once we get home? When are you planning to tell them?"

"First, we need to get a proper check-up," Purvi said, her voice tinged with a mix of excitement and nervousness. "I want to make sure everything is fine before we announce anything."

I nodded in agreement. "Yes, we should definitely get the confirmation from the doctor first."

The conversation drifted into silence for a moment as we each got lost in our thoughts. The auto rumbled on, the familiar sights of the city passing by us. It felt surreal to be back home, with such monumental news to share.

Finally, the auto pulled up to our stop. We unloaded our bags and stepped out, feeling a mix of exhaustion and exhilaration.

As we stepped into the house, I could feel the warmth and familiarity envelop us. Mom was already there, waiting eagerly. Her face lit up with a bright smile as she hurried over to greet us, taking some of our luggage to ease our burden.

"Welcome home!" she exclaimed, her eyes sparkling with joy.

We settled into the living room, letting the comfort of home sink in around us.

"Will you have Poha before chai or coffee?" Mom asked, her voice full of gentle, motherly concern.

Purvi, ever the chai lover, replied, "I'll just have chai, Mummy. Wait—I'll come with you to help in kitchen."

"You just got home. Take a moment to rest and freshen up—everything's almost ready," Mom said, waving her off with a smile.

"I'll take coffee, please," I added, already feeling the need for a caffeine boost after the long journey.

"I think I'll have both—Poha and coffee," Priya chimed in cheerfully.

Mom laughed, a twinkle in her eye. "Of course, dear. Both it is."

Despite the excitement bubbling within me, I noticed Purvi behaving as if it was just another ordinary day. I couldn't contain my impatience any longer.

"Mummy, can you sit down for a moment?" I asked, trying to keep my voice steady.

She looked at me, a bit puzzled, but obliged. "Sure, what is it?"

I glanced at Purvi, who nodded, giving me the green light to share our news. Taking a deep breath, I said, "Purvi might be pregnant."

For a moment, the room was filled with silence. Mom's expression didn't change much, but I could see the wheels turning in her mind. "Acha," she finally said, clearly taken aback and at a loss for words.

"Yes," I continued, trying to break through her shock. "We're going for a check-up today to get a proper confirmation."

Mom nodded slowly, still processing the information. "Okay," she said simply.

Priya, ever the curious one, couldn't help but ask, "You didn't guess it with our sudden arrival?"

Mom shook her head, a small smile forming on her lips. "No, I didn't think about this," she admitted, still somewhat lost in the moment.

"Let's call Papa," I suggested, handing Mom the phone.

She took a moment to gather her thoughts before making the call. "Hurry," I urged, excitement bubbling up again.

She dialled and, after a few rings, said, "They've reached home safely, and also, Purvi might be pregnant."

Papa's response was swift and to the point. "Okay, so that's why the sudden visit. That's good news. What now?"

"They'll go to the doctor for a proper check-up and confirmation," she replied.

"Let me know what the doctors says, and if they need anything," he said, ending the call on a practical note.

I couldn't help but think, "Wow, another unexpected reaction."

Purvi decided it was time to call her parents and share the news as well. She dialled her mother's number, her hands trembling slightly as she held the phone to her ear. She glanced at me, and I gave her an encouraging nod.

"Hello, Maa?" she said, her voice tinged with nervous excitement. "I have some news. I might be pregnant. We're going for a check-up today to confirm."

Her mother's response was immediate and filled with certainty. " I've been praying for this daily. I know it would happen soon."

Purvi was taken aback. She had expected a more enthusiastic congratulations rather than the calm assurance her mother gave. "Ok... thank you, Maa," she replied, a bit flustered.

Before she could say more, her father's voice came on the line. "Take care of yourself and your in-laws, beta, and let us know what the doctor says, send me the reports as well" he said warmly.

Purvi smiled, feeling a mix of emotions. "Thanks, Dad. We will. I'm just so nervous."

Her mother's voice softened. "I understand, dear. But trust me, everything will be fine. We're all here for you."

Purvi's eyes glistened with tears. "I know, Maa. It's just a lot to take in."

After a few more minutes of conversation, filled with both advice and reassurances, Purvi hung up the phone. She looked at me, her eyes filled with a mixture of relief and lingering anxiety.

"I thought they'd scream or cry or something," she chuckled. "That was... anticlimactic."

"Me too", I said and shared the laugh with her.

Whether it was the suddenness of the announcement or their overwhelming happiness, their reactions were not what we had anticipated. We had hoped for more excitement, but perhaps their joy was so deep that it left them momentarily speechless.

Papa took the doctor's appointment for 1 PM, and I also asked Mom to join us. She happily agreed. We got ready to go to the hospital. I took Purvi with me on the bike, while Papa dropped Mom at the hospital. As I navigated the streets, I tried to drive as slowly and carefully as possible, avoiding the potholes that dotted the road.

"Are you okay back there?" I asked, glancing at Purvi in the rearview mirror.

She smiled and squeezed my shoulder. "Yes, just a bit nervous."

At the hospital reception, they asked for some details, and I completed the formalities. They handed me a file and directed us to Room 2 for a preliminary checkup. As we approached the room, I noticed a handful of women waiting, all at various stages of their pregnancies.

Purvi and I found seats among them. The atmosphere was a mix of anticipation and calm. Two nurses were managing the pre-routine checkup activities, such as taking weights, blood pressure, and asking the usual questions about the last period date (LPD), the expected date, and any complications so far.

As we waited, I noticed Purvi fidgeting slightly. "How are you feeling?" I asked her softly.

"A bit nervous and anxious," she admitted.

After what felt like an eternity, it was our turn. The nurse called Purvi's name, and we walked into the room. The nurse was efficient, but kind, as she asked Purvi the routine questions and recorded her responses. She took Purvi's weight and blood pressure, and then asked her to take another pregnancy test. The result was still somewhat faint, but the nurse noted it in the file for the doctor to analyse.

"Everything looks normal so far," the nurse said, handing over the file to the doctor's assistant. "Please wait outside until the doctor calls you."

We returned to the waiting area. I was getting impatient, glancing at my watch every few minutes. "It's taking take so long," I muttered.

Purvi said in a calming tone. "This is just the beginning. Be prepared for more of this."

After an hour of waiting, that seemed to stretch on forever, we were finally called inside. "Purvi Shroff," the assistant called out, and we made our way into the doctor's cabin.

The room was adorned with certificates, degrees, and various pregnancy-related charts and models. The doctor, Doctor Mehta, knew us well, especially my mom. She greeted us warmly, making us feel at ease immediately.

"Hello Mrs. Shroff," Doctor said with a friendly smile. "How have you all been?"

"We're good, doctor. A bit anxious today," She admitted.

Doctor nodded understandingly as she looked over Purvi's file. After a brief review, she looked up with a beaming smile. "Congratulations, Purvi. You are pregnant."

A wave of relief and joy washed over me. I glanced at Purvi, who had tears of happiness in her eyes. "Finally, we got the confirmation we were waiting for," I whispered.

"But what about the blurry line on the test?" I asked, still a bit anxious.

"Yes, it happens sometimes," Doctor Mehta explained gently. "You're just entering the second month, so it's normal for the test lines to be faint."

"Thank you, doctor," Purvi said, her voice choked with emotion. "What should we do next?"

Doctor outlined the next steps, which included scheduling the first ultrasound and starting prenatal vitamins. "Make sure you get plenty of rest, eat a balanced diet, and avoid stress," she advised. "I'll see you back here in a few weeks for the ultrasound."

As we stepped out of the doctor's cabin, Mom looked at us with a proud, glowing smile.
"I knew it would be good news," she said, her voice filled with warmth.

"Mummy, you didn't seem that excited when we first told you," I teased gently.

She chuckled. "It was all so sudden—I didn't know how to react. And I was waiting for the doctor's confirmation to let it really sink in."

As we walked out of the hospital, I spotted Dad waiting near the gate, holding a box of sweets in his hands.

"Papa, you brought sweets?" I asked, surprised.

"Of course!" he said, smiling wide. "Your mom already called me. News like this needs a proper celebration—so here's a sweet start."

He opened the box and handed sweets to me and Purvi. Soon the unexpected reactions turned into unforgettable moments of happiness.

THIRD MONTH

The 3 Months Rule

We got home, our hearts still pounding with excitement from the doctor's confirmation. Purvi immediately decided she wanted to share the joyous news with everyone.

She reached for her phone, but Mom gently placed a hand on her arm—a silent reminder of tradition.

"Purvi," Mom said, her voice calm yet firm. "Be careful beta... In our tradition, we don't disclose this news to everyone except our close family until after the first three months."

Purvi looked a little taken aback but quickly nodded in agreement. "Alright, Mummy. I'll only tell my family then," she said, a hint of excitement still in her voice.

She first dialled her parents. The phone rang for a few moments before her mother answered.

Purvi could hardly contain herself. "Maa, Dad," she began, her voice trembling with excitement.

"What is it, Purvi?" her mother asked, a mixture of curiosity and concern in her voice.

"We're pregnant! The doctor just confirmed it. You're going to be *Nana* and *Nani!*" Purvi exclaimed, unable to hold back her joy any longer.

There was a brief silence before her mother's voice filled with pure elation. "Oh, Purvi, that's the best news we could have ever received! Congratulations, beta! We are so happy for you!"

Her father's voice joined in, equally thrilled. "This is wonderful news, Purvi! Take good care of yourself and the baby. We can't wait to meet our grandchild."

Tears of happiness welled up in Purvi's eyes. "Thank you, Dad. But please, don't tell anyone else until after the third month."

"Of course, we understand," her mother replied, her voice filled with emotion. "We won't say a word."

Next, Purvi called her younger brother, Chirag. "Hey, Chirag, guess what?" she teased, her tone playful.

"What is it, Jiji?" Chirag asked, sounding curious and a bit impatient.

"You're going to be *Mama* soon!" Purvi announced, her voice brimming with excitement.

"No way! That's amazing!" Chirag shouted, clearly over the moon. "I can't wait to be called Mama! Jiji, you need to take care of yourself and my nephew or niece, okay?"

"I will, Chirag," Purvi promised, laughing at his enthusiasm. "And remember, don't tell anyone else until the third month."

"Got it, Jiji." Chirag replied, his voice full of excitement.

Finally, Purvi called her sister, Ruchi. "Ruchi, I have some exciting news," Purvi said, her smile widening.

"What is it, Jiji?" Ruchi asked eagerly.

"We're having a baby!" Purvi shared, her eyes sparkling with joy.

Ruchi squealed with delight. "Oh my God! This is the best news ever! I'm already thinking of names. How about Pumpkin for a cute girl?"

Purvi laughed. "Let's not get ahead of ourselves, Ruchi. But Pumpkin... is adorable. And remember, no telling anyone until after the third month."

"Don't worry, Jiji. I won't say a word," Ruchi promised, her voice filled with excitement. But then, a slight pause followed.

"What's wrong?" Purvi asked, sensing something was up.

"Well," Ruchi hesitated, "I had my phone on speaker when you called, and my friends heard everything. They're so excited too!"

Purvi's eyes widened. "Oh, Ruchi! You weren't supposed to say anything yet!"

"I know, I know," Ruchi said quickly. "But it wasn't intentional, I promise! They just happened to be here when you called. And they're really good at keeping secrets, I swear!"

Purvi sighed but couldn't stay upset. "Alright, just make sure they don't spread it around. We need to stick to the tradition."

"I will, Jiji, I promise," Ruchi assured her, her voice earnest.

As Purvi hung up the phone, she let out a sigh of contentment. "Everyone is so happy," she said, leaning back against the couch, her eyes glistening with tears of joy.

We all were super excited, but somewhere deep inside, I could sense that Purvi was missing her work life. She had always been someone who thrived on the routine and challenges of her job. One evening, as we sat together on the couch, I noticed a hint of melancholy in her eyes.

"What's wrong, Purvi?" I asked gently.

She sighed, her shoulders slumping slightly. "I just miss my work, Aman. I know this is an important time, but I feel like a part of me is missing without my job. Sometimes I stare at the wall and imagine being at my desk—handling cash, joking with colleagues, dealing with customers. Funny how I hated it some days, and now I'd do anything to have it back for a little while."

I sat beside her and said reassuringly. "I understand, Purvi. But think of this as a temporary break. You can use this free time to focus on your hobbies, the things you love but never had enough time for."

She looked at me, a faint smile appearing on her lips. "You're right. I've always wanted to get back into drawing."

A spark of an idea lit up in my mind. "Wait here, I will be back in few minutes" I said, jumping up from the couch.

"Where are you going?" she asked, her curiosity piqued.

"You'll see," I replied with a grin, grabbing my keys and heading out the door.

I went to the local art supply store and spent some time carefully selecting a drawing book and a set of artist pencils. I knew how much Purvi loved to draw, and I hoped this would bring a smile to her face.

When I returned home, I found her sitting on the couch, looking a bit more relaxed. "Guess what I got?" I said, holding up the bag from the art store.

Her eyes widened with surprise and delight. "Oh, Aman! You didn't have to."

"I wanted to," I said, handing her the bag. "I thought this might help you channel your creativity and pass the time."

She took the bag and peeked inside, her face lighting up with joy. "Thank you so much! This is perfect."

I watched as she flipped through the empty pages of the drawing book and examined the pencils one by one, her excitement growing.

"I can't wait to start drawing again," she said, a little spark returning to her voice.

"Why not start now?" I suggested with a smile.

She laughed softly. "Not right now. I'm not quite in the mood. And I still have some household chores to finish."

"So, when will you start?" I asked.

"Soon... when I get some free time." She smiled, I nodded and didn't push her. She'd pick up the pencil when she was ready.

So far, there weren't any pregnancy symptoms like the ones we see in movies or hear about from others. You know how it usually goes in the movies: the girl feels like vomiting, rushes to the washroom, and then the elder ladies look around knowingly and congratulate everyone, announcing that the daughter-in-law is pregnant. But for Purvi, everything seemed normal—no cravings, no vomiting, no morning sickness. I have to admit, I was getting a little worried.

One evening, as we sat on the couch watching TV, I turned to Purvi. "It's strange, isn't it?" I asked. "You don't seem to have any of the usual symptoms."

She looked thoughtful for a moment before replying, "It's normal, I guess. I've read online—for some women, symptoms show up early, for some later. And in some cases, they hardly have any morning sickness or cravings at all, even throughout the pregnancy."

I nodded, though I couldn't shake the nagging worry at the back of my mind.

But it didn't last longer, in her seventh week, it happened. Purvi suddenly dashed to the bathroom, her hand over her mouth. I followed her, concerned. As I stood outside the bathroom door, I could hear the unmistakable sounds of her vomiting. Oddly, I felt a rush of relief.

When she finally emerged, pale and exhausted, I helped her back to the couch. "Are you okay?" I asked, handing her a glass of water.

She nodded weakly. "I guess it's starting."

My relief, however, was short-lived. Over the next few days, her vomiting increased from one or two times a day to three or four. Soon, she was vomiting after almost every meal. She could hardly manage to keep any food down, and it was clearly taking a toll on her.

One evening, as we sat down for dinner, she pushed her plate away after just a few bites. "I can't do this," she said, tears brimmed in her eyes. "I feel so sick all the time."

My mother, who was sitting with us, reached over and patted her hand gently. "It's normal to have vomiting until the end of the first trimester," she said reassuringly. "I had the same experience when I was pregnant with Aman."

Purvi nodded, though the exhaustion in her eyes didn't fade. "I told my mother, too," she said. "She said the same thing—that it's normal and that she had vomiting for all nine months."

I tried to offer some comfort. "At least we know it's normal. And we have an appointment with the doctor next week. We'll ask everything then, okay?"

She sighed deeply. "I just don't know whether to be relieved that it might end in three months or be worried that it could last the whole pregnancy."

In the days that followed, everyone tried to help in their own way. My mom started preparing fresh ginger tea twice a day, hoping it would settle her stomach. Purvi's mom, over countless phone calls, suggested home remedies like ajwain water, sucking on aam papad, having lemon juice with a pinch of salt, and even trying plain curd rice for dinner. A friend recommended chewing fennel seeds after meals, another suggested dry toast before getting out of bed. Someone even swore by peppermint tea.

But nothing seemed to provide lasting relief. Some things helped briefly, but the nausea always crept back. Still, Purvi braved through it—quietly, with the strength only she knew she had.

One afternoon, as I sat with Purvi in the living room, I could see how exhausted she was. "I feel so helpless," she said, her voice breaking. "I can't eat anything without feeling sick. I'm so tired all the time."

"We have an appointment next week for the first sonography. We'll ask the doctor about this. Maybe they can give us something to help."

She squeezed my hand weakly. "I hope so. I feel so drained, Aman."

Seeing her like this broke my heart. Purvi was always so full of life, and now she was struggling just to get through the day. I did everything I could to make her comfortable, from fetching her ginger tea to rubbing her back when she felt nauseous. But it never felt like enough.

One night, as we were getting ready for bed, I noticed she hadn't touched her dinner. "Purvi, you have to eat something," I said softly.

"I can't, Aman. The smell of food makes me feel sick," she replied, her voice barely above a whisper.

The next week couldn't come fast enough. The anticipation of the first sonography and the hope of finding some relief for Purvi's sickness kept us both on edge. We spent our evenings talking about what the sonography might reveal, trying to keep our spirits up.

"What do you think we'll see?" Purvi asked one night, her eyes lighting up at the thought.

"I'm not sure," I admitted. "But I read that we might be able to see the baby's heartbeat."

Her face softened with a smile. "That would be amazing."

That phase was a significant period of adjustment for us. However, it was especially challenging for Purvi, who faced both physical and mental challenges. She was very used to her work life and thoroughly enjoyed it. Suddenly having to leave everything behind and sit idle at home was a massive change for her, and she was not accustomed to it. On top of that, she was dealing with numerous physical changes. She couldn't eat properly and felt weak and tired due to constant vomiting. It was heartbreaking to see her struggling so much.

One evening, as we sat together on the couch, I noticed the deep fatigue in her eyes. "Purvi, you should try to eat something," I suggested gently.

She shook her head, looking dejected. "Aman, I can't even think about food without feeling nauseous. It's so frustrating."

I reached out and held her hand. "I know it's tough. But we need to find a way to make you feel better. Maybe we can try different foods or small portions."

She sighed. "I miss enjoying my favourite foods. Remember how I used to love peas? I could eat a whole kilogram by myself. And sweets! I had such a sweet tooth. Now, I can't even look at them."

I felt a pang of sadness. "It's so strange seeing you like this. You used to light up at the sight of your favourite foods."

"I know," she replied, her voice tinged with frustration. "It's like my body has betrayed me. Everything I used to love now makes me feel sick."

We sat in silence for a while, the weight of the situation settling between us. I could see how much she missed her old life, and it hurt to see her so unhappy.

"I understand," I said, feeling helpless. "We'll get through this, Purvi. It's just a phase, and things will get better."

She nodded, but I could see the doubt in her eyes. The physical changes were taking a toll on her, and it was hard to stay optimistic.

For Mom, Dad, and me, there was also a significant change in our lives. Mom and Dad previously lived in their own way, with a particular routine for waking up, eating lunch and dinner, and managing their day-to-day activities. But after Purvi's pregnancy news, they had to bring considerable changes to their lifestyle to accommodate her needs.

The first big change was the bedroom arrangement. Mom and Dad gave us their bedroom, shifting to another room so that Purvi could have the most comfort possible. It was a gesture that spoke volumes about their love and support. "Are you sure about this?" I asked them, feeling a bit guilty.

"Of course, Aman," Dad replied with a reassuring smile. "Purvi needs to be as comfortable as possible right now. We can manage in the other room."

Their whole schedule had to change. Previously, they woke up early, did some exercises, and had tea together. Dad would eat lunch early and then go to the shop, while Mom prepared dinner in the afternoon and then also headed to the shop. They used to have dinner very early, but now everything had to be adjusted.

"Papa, you don't have to change your routine so much," I suggested one morning as he packed his tiffin.

"It's okay, Beta," he said, patting my shoulder. "This is important. We all need to be flexible right now. Plus, I like taking my lunch with me now. It means I can spend more time at the shop and come home earlier."

Mom, who used to stay at the shop all day, now adjusted her schedule too. "I'll stay back and go later," she said one afternoon while we were discussing the new routine. "That way, I can help Purvi more during the day."

I could see how much they cared and how willing they were to adapt for the sake of Purvi and the baby. It was heartwarming and inspiring. "Thank you, Mummy," Purvi said one evening, her voice filled with gratitude. "I know this isn't easy for you."

"Nonsense, That's the least we can do for our Grandchild." Mom replied, hugging her gently.

Dinner time also shifted. They now had dinner after coming back from the shop, which was much later than they were used to.

Purvi, looking a bit tired but content, smiled. "We took the right decision coming home, I don't know if we could have managed this with you"

For me, it wasn't that tough since I had been working from home for the past two years due to COVID-19, so I didn't have much difficulty adjusting. However, with Purvi's pregnancy, I now had more responsibilities. The first and most important responsibility was taking care of Purvi. I tried to always be with her and make sure she was comfortable and well looked after.

"Aman, can you get me some water?" Purvi would ask, and I'd immediately get up to fetch it for her, making sure she had everything she needed.

"Aman, do you think I'm being too demanding?" Purvi asked one day, her eyes reflecting a mix of guilt and gratitude.

"Not at all, Purvi," I replied, giving her a reassuring smile. "Your comfort and health are the top priority right now. Just tell me whatever you need."

Apart from looking after Purvi, there was also the construction of our new house to consider. Every morning, Dad and I would visit the construction site to check on the development. Sometimes, Mom would join us if needed, but we avoided bringing Purvi along. The road to the site had many potholes, and we didn't want people around us to know that she was in Burhanpur. It was too early to disclose her pregnancy, as per the traditional three-month rule, and we didn't want to lie unnecessarily.

One morning, as Dad and I prepared to leave for the site, Purvi said, "I wish I could come with you. It would be nice to see the progress on our new home."

"I know, Purvi," I said, giving her a quick hug. "But it's best if you stay here and rest. The road is too bumpy, and we don't want to take any risks."

"I understand," she sighed, settling back into her chair. "Just take some pictures for me, okay?"

"Of course," I assured her.

At the construction site, Dad and I would discuss the progress with the workers and make decisions on various aspects of the build. "The foundation looks good," Dad noted one day, inspecting the work.

Balancing work, taking care of Purvi, and overseeing the construction was demanding, but it also brought a sense of purpose. Each day, I felt more connected to our future home and more committed to ensuring that everything was perfect for Purvi and our baby.

One evening, as we were discussing the construction progress, Mom mentioned, "You know, Aman, it's a good thing you're working from home. You can be here for Purvi whenever she needs you."

"Yes, Mummy," I replied. "COVID has affected so many lives in so many ways"

"Hope they don't call you to office soon" Purvi added, her eyes meeting mine.

I smiled. Thinking about what she said and hoping I can be with her and family in these times and shouldn't get call to office. But again, that's something I will have to worry tomorrow, and *I don't want to sacrifice today's moments in fear of tomorrow's thoughts.*

One morning, we received some very bad news. Someone in our very close family had passed away. The person was very dear to us, and the news hit us like a ton of bricks. We were all in a state of shock and heartbreak.

"We have to go and pay our respects," I said, looking at Purvi and my parents.

"Yes, of course," my father replied, his voice heavy with grief. "It's the least we can do for someone who was so close to us."

Purvi, sitting on the couch, looked torn. "I want to go too," she said softly. "But I know I can't."

As per Hindu customs, pregnant women are often advised not to attend funerals to protect the unborn from negative energy, both spiritual and emotional. Additionally, since we hadn't publicly announced her pregnancy yet due to the three-month tradition, explaining her absence was going to be tricky.

"I wish you could come," I told her, "But it's best for you and the baby if you stay home."

"I understand," she replied, her eyes filled with sorrow. "But what will we tell everyone? They'll surely ask about me."

"We'll have to lie," my mother said, shaking her head. "We don't have a choice. We'll say that you're not feeling well."

Purvi nodded in agreement.

When we arrived at the relative's house, the atmosphere was understandably heavy with grief. Family members and friends were gathered, offering their condolences and support.

"Aman, where is Purvi?" one of the relatives asked. "She couldn't make it?"

"No, she's not feeling well," I replied, trying to keep my voice steady. "She wanted to come, but she's resting at home."

"Oh, I see." the relative said, nodding sympathetically.

I nodded, feeling a pang of guilt for lying but knowing it was necessary.

Throughout the ceremony, I couldn't help but thought about Purvi at home. I knew she must be feeling isolated and upset that she couldn't be there to pay her respects. When we finally returned home, she was sitting in the living room, looking anxious.

"How did it go?" she asked, her voice trembling slightly.

"It was hard," I admitted, sitting down next to her. "Everyone was asking about you. We told them you weren't feeling well."

"I don't feel good lying to them, but we didn't have any other choice." Mom said expressing her guilt.

We nodded in agreement, as we knew we were not wrong as per the circumstances and situation.

And finally, the day arrived for our first sonography, also known as the dating scan. Being part of the modern generation, we had done our research using Google, trying to guess what would happen during the scan. We learned that we might see our baby for the very first time and that it would be around the size of a cherry. We were also excited about the possibility of hearing our baby's heartbeat.

That morning, as we got ready, the anticipation was palpable. "Are you ready for this?" I asked Purvi, trying to gauge her emotions.

"I am, but I'm also a bit nervous," she admitted.

"Everything will be fine." I said reassuring her.

We went to the hospital, a sense of anticipation hanging in the air. It was me, Purvi, and my mom. As we walked through the hospital doors, the usual process followed once we reached the reception. I paid the fees, while Purvi and my mom took seats in the waiting area. The receptionist handed us a few forms, and we filled them out with the necessary details. Soon, a nurse came to escort us to the examination room for the routine checkup.

In the room, Purvi's weight and blood pressure were measured. The nurse asked if there had been any complications or concerns. "I've been having a lot of vomiting lately," Purvi mentioned, her voice tinged with worry.

The nurse nodded sympathetically. "That's quite common in the first trimester. I'll make a note for the doctor," she said, jotting down the information in Purvi's file. "Just wait here for a bit; the doctor will see you soon."

We were directed back to the waiting area. I could see the anxiety building in Purvi's eyes as she glanced at the clock repeatedly. "It'll be our turn soon," I said, trying to keep my voice calm and steady.

Finally, Purvi's name was called. "Purvi, please come in for the sonography," the nurse announced. However, to my disappointment, only Purvi was allowed into the room for the scan. "You and your mother will need to wait outside," the nurse added.

As Purvi disappeared behind the door, I felt a pang of disappointment. "Why don't they let fathers in for these moments?" I muttered under my breath.

"Don't worry, Aman. She'll be out soon, and we will hear everything from the doctor," my mom said, patting my shoulder.

I paced the floor, each minute dragging on. I kept looking at the door, hoping to see Purvi emerge with good news. My mom tried to distract me with small talk, but my mind was solely focused on Purvi and the baby.

After what felt like a lifetime, Purvi finally came out. Her face was glowing with a mixture of relief and joy, like someone who had just been handed a precious gift. "How did it go?" I asked eagerly.

"They found the heartbeat!" she exclaimed, her eyes sparkling. "It was the most beautiful sound I've ever heard."

My heart leapt with joy. "Really? What did it sound like?"

"Like a rapid, steady thumping," she described, her smile widening. "So fast and strong. I can't believe it, Aman. Our baby is doing fine."

We were then called into the doctor's cabin. As we entered, the doctor greeted us warmly. "Everything looks normal," she began, addressing my mom.

"What about the vomiting?" Purvi asked, a hint of worry still in her voice. "It's mostly after eating meals."

The doctor nodded. "That's quite normal until the end of the first trimester. Most women experience this. Try eating light food, avoid uncooked and outside meals which can cause acidity, and increase your liquid intake. I'll also prescribe some medication to help with the nausea."

I felt a wave of relief wash over me. "Thank you, doctor," I said, my voice filled with gratitude. "We were quite worried."

The doctor smiled reassuringly. "It's all part of the process. Just take it easy and avoid lifting heavy objects or overexerting yourself."

As we left the doctor's cabin, I collected the prescribed medicines from the pharmacy. Purvi and I headed home on our bike, my mom waiting for my father to pick her up. The ride home was filled with excitement and relief.

On our way home, Purvi couldn't contain her excitement. She was practically glowing with joy, her eyes sparkling as she spoke. "Aman, I heard our baby's heartbeat!" she exclaimed, her voice full of wonder and happiness.

"Yeah?" I replied, my own excitement growing.

"Yes," she nodded enthusiastically, "it was the best sound I have ever heard. It wasn't like a normal heartbeat. It was something like bhap, bhap, bhap, and it was so fast."

"Our baby's heartbeat, Aman. Can you believe it?" she continued, her voice trembling with emotion. "I could listen to that sound all day."

I smiled, feeling a mix of joy and a twinge of jealousy. "I wish I could have heard it too," I said, my voice soft. "It must have been amazing."

"It was more than amazing," Purvi said, squeezing my hand. "It felt so real, so... alive. Our baby is growing, Aman. I can't wait for you to hear it at the next scan."

I nodded, feeling a little better. "I can't wait for that moment." "Yes, we did find the baby's heartbeat," I said.

Purvi sighed, navigating through the city streets. "I know the doctor said it's normal and that some women lose weight in the early stages of pregnancy, but it still worries me."

"I understand," I replied, "But the doctor did say it was normal to have these symptoms in first semester. And also, with this medication and proper diet you will definitely feel better."

Despite the doctor's reassurances, neither of us could fully relax. Like any other modern couple, we turned to social media for help. Instagram, in particular, seemed to know exactly what we were looking for, often suggesting content that aligned with our thoughts.

"In today's era, you can find a solution to almost any problem easily," I remarked, scrolling through my feed. "But the thing is, there are so many solutions that it becomes overwhelming."

"Exactly," Purvi agreed, looking at her phone. "On Instagram, we found so many remedies and diet charts suggested by influencers, Insta doctors, and other moms. It's just confusing."

"Most of them suggest a low acidic diet plan," I said, reading one of the posts. "Having smaller, more frequent meals, eating every two to three hours, and drinking plenty of fluids. And walks after meals"

"We've tried all of that, but nothing seems to help," Purvi said, her frustration evident. "I guess we just have to wait for the first trimester to be over."

I nodded, feeling a strange mix of helplessness and quiet determination. The first trimester was almost over, and we had tried nearly everything— what the doctor prescribed, what family and friends suggested, even remedies from Instagram reels. But nothing really worked. The nausea stayed, stubborn and constant.

Sometimes I'd try to look at the bigger picture and think, "*Three months are done... only six more to go.*" And then it would hit me—*in just six months, we'll have a baby.* That thought alone was overwhelming... but also kind of magical.

FOURTH MONTH

The Baby Bump

The doctor prescribed a regimen:

multivitamins, iron, and protein supplements thrice daily, milk powder, and weekly injections. Purvi had been diligently following it all.

One night, as she stirred the last of the protein powder into her milk before bed, she sighed, "Aman, this powder is almost finished. We'll need to buy more."

"We'll get it tomorrow; we have the doctor's appointment anyway," I replied.

"Yeah, but this time, let's get the chocolate flavour. I can't stand this elaichi one anymore."

"Sure, but don't forget the injection," I reminded her gently.

Her eyes narrowing as she recalled the prick of the last injection. "Ugh, you don't know how much it hurts. And that nurse... she treats me like I'm some animal."

I looked at her. "But you're handling it so bravely. I'm not sure I could endure all those injections and medicines."

She looked at me, her eyes soft yet determined. "I'm not brave, Aman. But I'm trying to be. I'm doing everything for this baby. Every pain, every sacrifice, every injection—it'll all be worth it when I see our baby's face for the first time. I can bear anything for that moment."

I was speechless. In that moment, I witnessed her transformation—from a carefree girl to a determined mother. It was awe-inspiring.

I guess it's true what they say—*a man becomes a father the day his child is born, but a woman steps into motherhood from the very first day of pregnancy.* From that moment on, everything changes for her—her body, her mind, her priorities. She's already nurturing, already sacrificing, already loving someone she hasn't even seen yet.

And watching Purvi go through it all... made me feel that truth more deeply than ever.

And soon it was time for our monthly checkup, and we headed to the doctor's clinic with a mix of anticipation and hope. Our primary concern at that point was Purvi's persistent vomiting and nausea. While we knew these symptoms were common during the first trimester, the fact that they hadn't eased by now made us slightly anxious.

As we entered the clinic, Purvi whispered, "I hope that this time doctor gives me something that actually helps with vomiting."

I chuckled softly, trying to lighten the mood. "Why? Aren't your Insta-doctors and Mr. Google helping you with this?!"

She shot me a playful glare but smiled anyway. "Very funny, Aman."

After waiting for our turn, we were finally called into the doctor's cabin. The doctor greeted us warmly. "How are you feeling, Purvi?" she asked, scanning her file.

"Still nauseous, doctor," Purvi replied, sounding exasperated. "The vomiting just doesn't seem to stop."

The doctor nodded empathetically. "That's quite common until the third month, but since it's continuing, I'll prescribe some specific meds for some relief. It should help settle your stomach."

Purvi let out a small sigh of relief. "Thank you, doctor. I just want to feel normal again."

The doctor smiled and then said, "Now this is your new normal, also, it's time for your first NT scan. This scan is crucial to assess the baby's development. Here's the prescription for it."

We were well aware of the NT scan, especially with our Instagram feeds constantly flooded with pregnancy-related content. It was almost as if the algorithm knew exactly what we were going through, showing us reels tailored to our current trimester and situation. In many ways, it felt like a parenting guidebook—covering everything from baby names to prenatal scans. Like the NT scan is an early pregnancy ultrasound, typically performed between 11 and 13 weeks of pregnancy that checks the baby's neck to help spot the risk of Down syndrome or other health issues.

As we walked out of the clinic, prescription in hand, Purvi looked at me with a renewed sense of hope. "I can't wait for the scan," she said. "I'll get to hear the heartbeat again and see our tiny baby."

I smiled back, feeling the same anticipation. "Absolutely," I replied. "I'll book the appointment."

Apart from managing the changes that pregnancy brought, we had another major task at hand— wrapping up everything in Umaria and vacating the house. It wasn't just a chore; it felt like closing a significant chapter of our lives. To tackle this, I decided to go with Chirag, my brother-in-law, who was visiting Umaria for the first time.

We arrived at the small but charming station of Umaria in the early morning. As soon as I stepped out, a wave of nostalgia hit me. The place had a simplicity that I had grown fond of over the years—familiar faces, fewer crowds, and a slower pace of life.

"Wow, so this is Umaria," Chirag said, looking around with curiosity. "It's peaceful here, unlike the chaos of big cities."

"Exactly," I replied with a smile. "It's small, but it's peaceful and calm."

I decided to capture every moment on my phone, from the rustic station platform to the autorickshaw stand, where I spotted the familiar "auto bhaiya" I'd often hired. They waved at me, their faces lighting up in recognition.

As we rode through the streets toward the house, I couldn't resist filming the roads, the tiny shops, and the landmarks I had passed countless times. "This place has so many memories," I said to Chirag, feeling a little sentimental.

"Leaving all this must be hard, right, Jijaji?" Chirag said, eyes scanning the quiet streets.

"It was," I admitted. "But life moves on."

When we finally reached the house, I opened the gate, half-expecting a dusty mess. To my surprise, it wasn't as bad as I had imagined.

"This doesn't look too bad," Chirag said, surveying the house.

"I know, right? Less cleaning, more packing!" I replied, relieved.

Without wasting any time, we got straight to work. We had only one day to pack everything, vacate the house, and complete a few errands. Our first task was separating the clothes.

"Alright, let's sort these into 'take' and 'leave' piles," I said, opening the first cupboard.

Chirag laughed. "I guess Jijaji we might want Jiji's opinion for this."

"Already on it," I replied, pulling out my phone to video call Purvi.

As the call connected, Purvi's face lit up on the screen. "How's it going, guys, Chirag are you liking it there, how's the place?" she asked.

"Good so far, peaceful, but we're stuck on the clothes," Chirag admitted.

For the next hour, Purvi gave detailed instructions, from which things to pack to which winter clothes to leave behind. Chirag joked, "Jiji, I didn't know you have so many clothes.'"

Purvi laughed, "It's not many, just few... for every occasion."

Once the clothes were sorted, we moved on to utensils, blankets, and other essentials. It was a surprisingly smooth process, and by noon, we were done with most of the packing.

"Time for a break, also I am hungry" I declared, wiping sweat from my forehead.

We freshened up and ordered lunch from a nearby restaurant. The food arrived quickly, and we sat on the floor, eating from paper plates amidst a sea of packed boxes.

"So Jijaji, is this the only restaurant here" Chirag joked, biting into a paratha.

"If you can call this place restaurant then yes!" I replied, laughing.

By the time lunch was over, we realized we had wrapped up everything much earlier than expected. Exhausted but with some free time, we decided to take a power nap.

"Let's recharge for an hour," I suggested, as we spread the blanket.

"Good idea, Jijaji" Chirag agreed, already lying down. "We have almost completed the major tasks."

As I lay down, I couldn't help but reflect on how smoothly the day had gone so far. Leaving Umaria was bittersweet, but having Chirag's company and Purvi's involvement made it easier.

I was tired, but sleep avoided me. My mind kept wandering back to all the moments Purvi and I had shared in Umaria, the life we had built together, and the memories we had created. And then it struck me—what if I made a farewell video for Purvi? A video filled with all the places, routines, and moments that had been a part of our lives here. The idea excited me, and I instantly began making mental notes of everything I needed to capture for this little surprise.

By the time I was done planning, it was 5 PM. The sunlight was fading, and I knew I had to hurry if I wanted good footage. I turned to Chirag, who was snoring softly beside me, and shook him awake.

"Chirag, get up! We've got work to do!"

"Huh? What work Jijaji?" he mumbled groggily.

"I'll be making a farewell video for Purvi. We need to go out and start filming before it gets dark," I explained.

"That's a great idea Jijaji" he said, rubbing his eyes.

We got ready and headed out. I kept my phone ready, recording everything that had been a part of our daily life.

"This is the kirana shop where we used to buy groceries," I narrated as I filmed.

Chirag chimed in, "And the shopkeeper always greet Jiji as Madam ji right?"

"Exactly!" I said, smiling at the memory.

We moved on to the spot where we had taken countless late-night walks, our quiet escape to talk about everything and nothing. The railway crossing came next, with its familiar clanging bell and the wait for trains to pass.

"Do you remember how Purvi would always video call you guys from here?" I laughed, pointing the camera at the crossing.

"Yes, and make us see trains" Chirag joked.

We continued to the vegetable market and the dairy shop, capturing the places that had become second nature in our routine. Finally, we arrived at Purvi's bank.

As we walked in, we were greeted with warm smiles and a flurry of excitement. "Aman sir! So good to see you!" one of Purvi's colleagues exclaimed. I introduced them to Chirag.

"Meet Chirag, Purvi's brother." I said pointing to Chirag.

"They've been missing Purvi a lot," I whispered to Chirag.

We distributed sweets, and decided to video call her so everyone could see her. As the call connected, Purvi's face lit up on the screen.

"Hi, everyone!" she said, waving enthusiastically.

Her colleagues waved back, some getting emotional. "We miss you so much, Purvi

Madam" one of them said, tears welling up in her eyes.

"I miss you all too," Purvi replied, her voice soft with emotion.

Once the call ended, I whispered to Chirag, "Now comes the tricky part—getting farewell messages from everyone for the video."

"Leave it to me, Jijaji" he said confidently.

Chirag worked his magic, convincing each person to share a heartfelt message for Purvi. It was beautiful—funny anecdotes, heartfelt goodbyes, and warm wishes for her future. I couldn't have asked for more.

"Purvi Madam made even Mondays bearable. Who's going to fight with the customers now?" said Atul sir, everyone laughed on the nostalgic moment.

As we wrapped up at the bank, I felt a sense of accomplishment. The video was coming together perfectly.

Back at the house, we finished packing up the remaining items. Some furniture was sold to the landlord, while a few essentials like utensils and blankets were packed to be couriered later. And recorded our last part of farewell video.

The camera panned from the cluttered kitchen to the scribbled wall calendar—her neat handwriting circling festival dates. *The silence in the background said more than any farewell message.*

Before leaving, we visited our favourite neighbours, Madhu and Vibha. They had been like family to us, always there in times of need.

"We'll miss you both so much," Madhu said, her voice tinged with sadness.

"Don't forget to call us often," Vibha added.

"We won't," I promised. "Thank you for everything. You've been the best neighbours we could've asked for."

Finally, it was time to say goodbye. As we locked the door for the last time, I paused, taking in the house one last time.

"This place gave us some of our best memories." I admitted to Chirag.

This wasn't just a house we were leaving. It was the place where we learned to build a life—one grocery trip, one chai, one argument at a time.

As the train pulled out of the station, I couldn't help but feel a pang of sadness. Leaving Umaria wasn't just about moving to a new place; it was leaving behind a part of us.

"You don't know you're living your golden days until you start packing them in cardboard boxes," I said, half to myself.

Chirag nodded. "But the memories will always stay with you."

And he was right. Umaria, its people, and the life we had built there would always hold a special place in our hearts. The farewell video was my way of keeping those memories alive—not just for Purvi, but for both of us.

Chirag left for Ujjain after spending a couple of days with us, leaving the house quieter than before. Life resumed its usual rhythm, centered around our pregnancy routine. Yet, a significant milestone loomed on the horizon—the NT scan.

We had booked an appointment at Apple Hospital, as suggested by our doctor.

Purvi, sitting behind me on the bike, let out a small sigh. "I hope everything goes fine"

"Don't overthink, Purvi. The doctor said it's just a routine check." I said reassuringly.

We reached the hospital at 11 AM sharp. The parking lot was already bustling, and the sight of families waiting, couples holding hands like nervous teenagers, and new fathers pacing like tensed cricket captains during a run chase, and the occasional sound of a baby crying painted a picture of life's many stages. After making the payment at the reception, we were directed to the ground floor, where all the scans were conducted.

The ground floor was a different world—quiet yet buzzing with purpose. Two receptionists managed the counters, verifying details and ensuring that all patients adhered to their timelines. Every scan, we learned, had a specific window during the pregnancy.

"Good morning," one of the receptionists greeted us with a polite smile. "Please provide your doctor's prescription and identification."

Purvi handed over the prescription while I took out my wallet for our Aadhar cards. "Here's the original," I said confidently, only to be met with a raised eyebrow.

"Sir, we need photocopies of your Aadhar cards," she explained.

It hit me—we had forgotten to bring copies. "I didn't know they were necessary," I admitted, feeling a little embarrassed.

"It's a mandatory document for every scan," she clarified, her tone firm but kind.

I sighed, glancing at Purvi, who looked equally concerned. The hospital was located on the outskirts of the city, and finding a Xerox shop nearby seemed impossible. I didn't want to leave Purvi alone, especially in her condition.

"I'll call Papa," I decided.

Within seconds, I was on the phone with my father. "Papa, can you please bring photocopies of our Aadhar cards to Apple Hospital? It's urgent."

His response was immediate. "Of course, beta. Give me 15 minutes."

"He is coming" I said smiling softly.

Sometimes we neglect the efforts of father, who will always go any extra miles for his children, who will always choose their luxuries above his own necessities.

True to his word, my father arrived with the copies in no time. Without saying a word, Papa handed over the photocopies. No drama, no *gyaan*. Just quiet strength—like always. Fathers show love in EMI instalments, I thought.

We submitted the documents, only to be told by the receptionist, "It might take another two hours for your turn."

Purvi and I exchanged frustrated looks. "Two hours?" I echoed, hoping she was mistaken.

"Yes, sir. It's a busy day," she said apologetically.

Left with no choice, we settled into the waiting area. The first five minutes dragged on endlessly, making two hours feel like an eternity.

"Let's play a game," she suggested, pulling out her phone, trying to lighten the mood.

"I'm not in the mood," I muttered, staring blankly at the wall.

"Come on, don't be a bore," she teased, giving me a playful nudge. "I'll let you win this time, okay?"

I looked at her, smirked, and shook my head. "Huh, in your dreams. Bring it on."

We played a couple of mobile games, she lied as mostly she won, watched some funny videos on Instagram, and even tried browsing through old photos to pass the time. At one point, we decided to take a walk around the hospital.

"Look at us," Purvi said with a wry smile, "'Trying everything we can to kill time, huh?"

"Better than staring at the walls," I teased.

Even with all our efforts, an hour crawled by. I couldn't help myself—I approached the receptionist again. "Any chance our turn is coming up soon?" I asked, throwing in a sad, hopeful expression.

She shook her head sympathetically. "Not yet, sir."

Defeated, I returned to Purvi. "No luck."

Finally, after what felt like ages, Purvi's name was called. A nurse guided her into the scanning room, leaving me outside.

I hadn't anticipated how anxious I would feel during this wait. The past two hours suddenly seemed like a breeze compared to these agonizing minutes. I tapped my foot, checked the time every few seconds, and even found myself biting my nails—a habit I had given up years ago.

When Purvi emerged from the room, my heart leapt. I rushed to her side.

"How did it go?" I asked, barely able to contain my nerves.

She smiled, her eyes shining with relief. "The doctor said everything is normal. Nothing to worry about."

Just five words, but they felt like *Hanuman ji* himself had lifted the mountain off my chest.

A wave of relief swept over me, and I exhaled deeply. "Thank God."

Though we were yet to collect the formal report, those words were all I needed. Still, curiosity got the better of us. Once we received the reports, we immediately started analysing them on our own.

Purvi held the papers close, pointing to each parameter. "Looks, everything's within range," she noted, her tone both relieved and proud.

But her smile faltered as she spotted one parameter near the boundary limit. "Is this okay?

It's on the edge," she murmured, her voice tinged with worry.

"Purvi, come on—we heard it straight from the doctor. You're fine. We're fine," I reminded her.

"I know," she said, scrolling through her phone.

Our ride home was filled with her surfing the internet for additional reassurance. "Mom said not to overthink," she said after a phone call with her mother.

"But still you will be looking, I know" I said, smiling.

By the time we reached home, Purvi was visibly calmer. "It's possibly nothing," she said.

"It's definitely nothing," I replied.

That day, amidst the waiting, worry, and relief, we realized that this journey was not just about bringing a new life into the world—it was also about growing into the roles of parents, one step at a time.

In every parenting journey, there's always that one person who takes on the role of "the expert." You know, the one who reads articles, watches endless videos, and dives into the rabbit hole of advice columns. In our case, that person was me.

If there was a video about the importance of eating leafy greens during the first trimester, I had seen it. If there was an article about the ideal sleeping position for a pregnant woman, I had read it. My Instagram feed was an endless parade of "what to eat in the first trimester," "exercises for a healthy pregnancy," and "how to bond with your baby before birth." Thanks to the Instagram algorithm, once it knew I was interested, there was no going back. My entire feed became a one-stop pregnancy advice column.

"Purvi," I'd call out enthusiastically, holding up my phone. "Did you know that walnuts are a great source of omega-3 fatty acids and help in the baby's brain development?"

She would roll her eyes and smirk. "Really, Sirji?"

Sirji—that was my new name, bestowed lovingly by Purvi and my family. It started as a joke when one day, after yet another one of my lectures about the benefits of hydration during pregnancy, my mom chuckled and said, "Before we do anything, let's consult Sirji."

Even though they poked fun at me, I knew my efforts were appreciated—at least sometimes. And moreover, the nausea and vomiting finally seemed to be in control. Whether it was the doctor's medicines, my constant suggestions, her diet plan, or simply the pregnancy reaching a more stable phase—we didn't really care. What mattered most was that Purvi could finally eat something without immediately throwing up.

Of course, it wasn't like she started enjoying her favourite dishes or having full meals. Most foods still made her feel uneasy. So, we stuck to the basics—raw tomatoes with a sprinkle of sugar, plain chapati, curd roti, dal roti, and lots of coconut water. It wasn't much, but it was something. And honestly, at that point, something was better than nothing. We didn't push her to eat anything "nutritious" or heavy, because every time we tried, it backfired— sometimes ending in another round of vomiting.

"Are you sure you don't want anything else?" I asked, looking at her plate that had nothing but a few raw tomato slices and a chapati.

"No, Aman," she said, gently shaking her head. "I don't feel like eating anything else. This is enough for me."

"Beta, little bit halwa at least? *Ghar ka bana hai?*" Mom asked from the kitchen.

"No, Mummy," Purvi replied softly.

"Okay, beta. Eat whatever you want," Mom said kindly, careful not to pressure her.

We all knew—comfort came first.

The second trimester truly feels like a magical phase in pregnancy. It's the time when the baby bump becomes more pronounced, making it clear to the world that something beautiful is happening. The first three months were full of uncertainties and adjustments, but now, with the growing bump, everything feels more real and tangible.

One evening, Purvi and I sat on the couch, talking about the changes she was experiencing. She rested her hand on her belly, gently caressing it.

"Do you feel it?" she asked, her eyes sparkling with a mix of curiosity and excitement.

"Feel what?" I asked, leaning closer.

"The baby. It's hard to explain, but it's like this little bump is my entire world now. I can't stop thinking about her."

I raised an eyebrow. "Her? What makes you so sure it's a girl?"

She smiled confidently. "I just know. Call it a mother's intuition or whatever you like"

"Hmm, so it's not a boy?" I teased. "You're ruling that out entirely?"

"Absolutely," she said, her lips curling into a playful smirk, eyes gleaming with mischief. "It's a girl. No doubt about it."

I said teasing her, shaking my head. "Okay, Ms. Psychic. If you're so sure it's a girl, then we already have her name."

She raised an eyebrow, a hint of mock surprise in her voice. "Wait, we haven't talked about this, have we?" She tilted her head, her gaze sharp, teasing.

"Of course, we have! Don't tell me you've forgotten." I leaned in, trying to suppress a grin, enjoying this little game.

She stared at me blankly, her expression shifting to one of playful confusion. "When? What did we decide?"

I gave her a knowing look, nudging her memory. "Your favourite movie," I prompted, letting the anticipation build.

She furrowed her brows, lips pursed in concentration. *Which one?!* she seemed to think, the wheels turning in her head. "I have so many," she mumbled, half-laughing, half-frustrated. "Think, think!"

"Yeh Jawani... I don't think Lara will suit her," she added with a mischievous smile, then paused. "And Naina is too common."

I leaned back, smirking. "Your favourite Gujarati movie. Now that's all the hint I can give."

Her eyes lit up, a spark of realization flickering across her face. "*REVA!*"

I nodded, grinning. "Yup. You were obsessed with that movie, and the name just stuck with us."

"I love it," she said softly, her hand still resting on her belly. "Reva meaning Maa Narmada River. It's perfect."

From that day on, we decided on the baby girl's name: Reva.

One afternoon, I heard Purvi laughing uncontrollably on a phone call, her voice echoing through the room as she lay on the bed, giggling like a teenager.

"Who is it?" I asked softly, curious but not interrupting her moment.

She turned the screen toward me with a wide grin—*Roopali Di*, her cousin sister. That explained the burst of laughter. The two of them were always a riot together, and now with pregnancy as a shared topic, there was no stopping them.

"You told her about your pregnancy?" I asked once the call ended, settling beside her.

"Yup, it's already three months now, I can say it freely. I also checked with Mummy," she said, still smiling.

"So, what were you laughing so hard about?" I asked, raising an eyebrow.

"Nothing much... just random gossips," she said casually. "She asked for baby bump photos, and then you know... girl talk."

She paused, trying to hold back another laugh. "Also, she sounded *so* happy when I told her. And also, she said... now that you're pregnant, you should start keeping distance from Aman Ji," she added with a naughty grin.

I laughed too.

As the days passed, Purvi's bump continued to grow, drawing more attention from friends and family. Every visit became an opportunity for others to comment on her glowing face or growing belly.

One day, Neha Aunty came over, carrying a box of homemade sweets, her warm smile lighting up the room. She looked at Purvi and said with a twinkle in her eyes, "You're glowing, beta! I can see the happiness shining through you."

Purvi chuckled softly, her cheeks flushing with a gentle pink. "Thank you, Aunty," she replied, her smile warm and grateful.

Neha Aunty's eyes sparkled with curiosity as she leaned in slightly. "So, what are you craving? Any specific food—sweet, spicy, or sour?"

Purvi shrugged, her smile fading a bit, replaced by a thoughtful look. "To be honest, I don't feel like eating much. People have cravings and all, but nothing for me."

Neha Aunty nodded understandingly, her face softening with sympathy. "Yeah, don't be bothered, beta. It happens to some people. It's all part of the journey."

Every evening, Purvi would talk to the baby bump, lovingly calling her Reva. It became her little ritual—a quiet, tender moment just between them. Whether she was sharing the highlights of her day, reading aloud her WhatsApp messages with dramatic flair, or singing soft lullabies, the name Reva added an extra layer of warmth, making those moments feel like a secret bond only they shared.

One evening, as she gently rubbed her belly, I teased her, "You know it could be a boy, right? And you're always treating the baby like it's a girl."

She rolled her eyes, her lips twitching with a playful smirk. "You're not thinking of any baby boy names? What should I do? You're always watching *Taarak Mehta*, just sometimes you can talk to the baby also!"

I laughed. "But what to say? It's your stomach."

She leaned in, her voice dropping to a whisper as if the baby could hear her. "The baby can listen! Say anything—or sing anything."

I sighed dramatically, then, with an exaggerated tone, began, "Umm... *Taarak Mehta ka Oolta Chashma, Taarak Bhai...*"

She burst into laughter, shaking her head. "Okay, that's enough for today."

Even though the journey ahead was still full of unknowns, one thing was certain: Our Baby was already the centre of our universe. And we couldn't wait to meet it.

FIFTH MONTH

Girl or Boy

Pregnancy was undoubtedly the centerpiece of our lives at that moment, but there was another monumental event unfolding simultaneously—our new home's construction. It was a dream we had been nurturing for years, and now it was on the verge of completion. Excitement, anxiety, and a never-ending to-do list had become our daily companions.

One quiet evening, as we sat on the couch with our feet up, Purvi leaned back, gently resting a hand on her growing belly. Her eyes softened with a dreamy look. "I still can't believe we're about to move into our own house," she said, her voice filled with awe and a little disbelief.

I nodded, my eyes glued to the latest construction photos on my phone. "Yeah... but there's still so much left to finish. We've got less than three weeks before the Vastu Puja. It honestly feels like we're racing against time."

"What's still pending?" she asked, a slight furrow appearing on her brows.

"Umm... quite a few things," I admitted. "Last-minute furniture finishing, tap fittings, whitewash touch-ups—and the Mandir mural painting. All of it is happening together, and though everything should wrap up in time, I'm a bit worried about the mural."

She smiled knowingly. "It'll get done. I'm sure of it. You're too impatient to let anything miss a deadline."

I raised an eyebrow. "Wait... was that a compliment? Is it a good thing or bad?"

She grinned, her tone playful. "It's a good thing when you apply it to others. But not so great when I'm the one on your target."

I burst into laughter, not even trying to defend myself—because she wasn't wrong. "Fair point."

Then I kept my phone aside and looked at her. "Alright, now enough about timelines and checklists. You just focus on resting and taking care of yourself... and the little one."

"Okay, but what do *you* want Girl or Boy?" she pressed, her gaze locking onto mine.

"Again! I've told you a hundred times—I don't have a preference. I'll be happy with either."

She rolled her eyes, clearly unsatisfied with my neutral stance. "That's such a boring answer. Pick one! Boy or girl?"

After a moment of hesitation, I sighed and gave in. "Fine, a boy."

Her reaction was immediate. She sat upright, her eyebrows shooting up. "Why? Why not a girl? Girls are so much better!"

I laughed at her sudden defensiveness. "You keep asking me over and over, so I just picked one to make you happy. You want a girl, so I thought I'd balance it out by saying boy."

"That's a stupid reason!" she exclaimed, crossing her arms. "Tell me the real reason you want a boy."

I tried to stifle a grin. "There is no real reason. I just said boy because you kept asking."

"Well, you better have a good explanation ready," she said, narrowing her eyes. "Because I'm going to tell this to the boy when he's born."

The next few days were a whirlwind of activity. Me and Dad visited the site daily to supervise the finishing touches—the final coat of paint, the installation of light fixtures, and the placement of tiles.

Sometimes, Dad would stay late with his lunch packed, while Mom took care of the shop. It became part of our routine. Most of the time, Mom, Dad, and I would visit the site to track the progress and discuss a few things. Occasionally, Purvi would also join us.

One quiet afternoon, as I walked through the nearly finished house, I called Purvi over video. The rooms were finally taking shape, and I couldn't wait to show her the updates.

"Look at this," I said, flipping the camera to the living room. "What do you think of the TV unit placement?"

She squinted at the screen, tilting her head slightly. "Hmm... it looks nice, but can you move it a little to the left? It's not perfectly aligned with the sofa."

I smiled, already signalling the electrician. "Anything else, boss?" I teased, enjoying her eye for detail even from a distance.

She grinned. "Yes, come home soon. We are missing you"

I raised an eyebrow. "We!?"

She gently placed a hand on her belly and smiled softly. "Me and the baby."

And just like that by the time the house was ready for the Vastu Puja, we all were exhausted but elated. Walking through the finished rooms, imagining our future as a family within those walls, made all the stress worth it. It wasn't just a house—it was the home where our dreams, laughter, and love would flourish.

With everything going on—the house construction, work, and of course, the pregnancy—it was time for our monthly visit to the doctor. This visit felt a little different, though. For one, Purvi's nausea and vomiting had significantly reduced compared to the previous month. Her energy levels were better, and her appetite had slowly started improving. It was a relief to see her eat a full meal without the grimace that usually followed. While some women experience nausea throughout their pregnancy, for others, it tends to subside as the body adjusts.

"Are you ready, madam?" I asked as Purvi sat in front of the mirror, tying her hair.

"Almost," she replied, her eyes lingering on her reflection. Then, softly, "Do you think I'll be a good mother?"

I paused for a moment, catching the vulnerability in her voice. "Yes," I said gently. "Why do you ask?"

She looked down, fiddling with her hair tie. "I don't know... I just feel so careless sometimes. I can't even take care of myself properly."

I moved closer and sat beside her. "With the baby, it'll be different. *when you are pregnant it's not just the baby growing inside you but also you growing into motherhood,* and besides, the way you care for Ruchi and Chirag, and how they're afraid of you–That's nothing short of being a mom already."

She cracked a smile. "Hmm... wait... they're not afraid of me at all."

"You're right," I said, grinning. "We all are!"

She burst out laughing and gave me a playful pat on the shoulder.

We reached the clinic on time and met the doctor. She asked about Purvi's health and the progress over the past month. "It's good to hear that the nausea and vomiting have reduced," she said, making notes on her tablet. "Your diet is improving too, so that's a great sign."

Purvi nodded. "Yes, but I still feel tired easily."

"That's normal," the doctor reassured her. "Your body is working overtime to support the baby. Continue with the same medications, and don't forget to hydrate."

Before we left, the doctor had a few new suggestions. "Have you heard about Garbh-Sanskar courses?" she asked, looking at us.

Although we had already read about it from Instagram, I tilted my head in curiosity. "Not really. What's that?"

"It's a set of practices—music, meditation, and readings—designed to promote the well-being of both the mother and the baby. It's based on ancient principles, and many couples find it beneficial. It might also be a good bonding activity for you two," she explained.

The doctor handed us a pamphlet. "You can explore the options here. They even have online sessions, so you don't have to travel."

We thanked her and were about to leave when she added, "Oh, and don't forget your next scan—the anomaly scan. It's crucial to ensure everything is developing as it should be."

Later that evening, while discussing the next steps, Purvi said, "What do you think about the GarbhSanskar course? Should we try it?"

I nodded. "Why not? If it helps you relax and is good for the baby, I'm all in."

The next day, we scheduled our anomaly scan at All Is Well Hospital, a place known for its advanced facilities. The booking process was surprisingly simple. I sent a photo of the doctor's prescription via WhatsApp, and within minutes, we had a confirmed slot for the next day.

"Wow, that was easy," I said, showing Purvi the confirmation message.

She smiled. "Finally, something that doesn't involve waiting in endless lines"

The next day started with a confirmation call from the hospital. "Are you coming for the scan today?" the receptionist asked.

"Yes, we're already on our way," I replied. "We'll be there in about 10-15 minutes."

Purvi sat behind me, nervously scrolling through her phone. "I hope everything goes smoothly," she murmured.

"It will," I reassured her. "This is just routine. We've got this."

Upon reaching the hospital, we quickly submitted all the required documents. Since we had inquired about the necessary paperwork earlier, we came prepared. The receptionist asked for Purvi's identity card, checked the details, and then motioned toward the waiting area.

"Please have a seat," she said politely. "Your turn will come soon."

Surprisingly, the wait wasn't as long as I'd expected. A nurse came to guide Purvi into the scan room. I instinctively stood up, ready to accompany her, but the nurse stopped me.

"Sorry, sir, only the patient is allowed inside," she said with a gentle smile.

I nodded and sat back down, watching as Purvi disappeared behind the door. The waiting felt endless, even though it was only 20-25 minutes.

When I saw Purvi walk out, her face wasn't the picture of relief I had hoped for. Instead, she looked concerned.

"What happened?" I asked immediately, my heart sinking.

"They couldn't capture all the parts," she said, her voice tinged with frustration. "The baby wasn't in the right position."

I tried to stay calm for her. "That's okay. It's common in these scans. Sometimes the baby just doesn't cooperate. We'll wait and try again."

The nurse advised Purvi to walk around for 15-20 minutes and, importantly, not to pee. As she paced the hospital corridors, she muttered, "This is torture. I really need to go!"

After some time, she couldn't hold it any longer. "I have to ask them," she said. She approached the receptionist and explained her situation. The receptionist made a quick call to the doctor and then nodded.

"You can go in now," she said.

I stayed back again, waiting patiently. This time, the scan took about 20 minutes. When Purvi returned, I noticed the same worried expression.

"Not again," I said, more to myself than her.

"They still couldn't get all the images," she admitted, sighing heavily.

We repeated the process for a third time, but the results were the same. By then, it was nearly 4 PM. We had arrived at the hospital at 11 AM, and the exhaustion was beginning to show on both our faces.

Finally, the doctor decided to call Purvi in for a fourth attempt, and this time, they invited me into the room as well. My heart raced with anticipation as I followed the nurse inside. It was the first time I would see our baby, hear its heartbeat—my excitement and curiosity peaked with each step. I couldn't help but imagine what it would look like, influenced by the countless reels and posts I'd seen on Instagram.

As we entered, the doctor gestured toward a small monitor. "There's your baby," she said.

I squinted at the screen, trying to make sense of the gray, grainy image. There was movement, but I couldn't quite connect it to the idea of a baby.

"Do you see it?" the doctor asked, smiling.

"Uh... kind of?" I replied hesitantly.

Purvi laughed softly. "It's harder to interpret than we thought."

"Doctor, can we listen to the heartbeat?" She asked.

"Yes, sure," doctor replied, adjusting the settings.

And then, that sound—the heartbeat. It wasn't just a rhythmic pulse; it felt like the baby was trying to speak to me. *It wasn't melodious music or an instrumental masterpiece, but it was the sound that you can hear for the rest of your lives.* There will be some special moments in father's life, some he can explain but mostly he can't, this is one of those moment.

The doctor continued the scan, capturing as many details as possible. After what felt like it dragged on endlessly, she finally said, "Alright, we've got most of what we need. That's all for today."

Before we left, Purvi couldn't resist asking, "Is everything okay?"

She replied casually, "It seems fine, but there are a few things we'll need to monitor closely."

She pointed at the scan results, where the acronym EIF (echogenic intracardiac focus) was highlighted in bold. "It's a small spot we sometimes see on the heart during scans," she explained. "It's often harmless and could resolve on its own, but we'll keep an eye on it. It's not uncommon, but we'll need to monitor it in future scans just to be sure."

Her tone was casual, but her words hit us like a ton of bricks. We exchanged a quick glance, both of us now deeply worried.

On the way home, Purvi stayed silent, I tried to ease the tension, my voice uncertain. "It's probably nothing. Doctors have to be thorough—that's their job."

She nodded but didn't say anything.

Once we got home, we couldn't shake the unease. Purvi made the mistake of Googling the doctor's words, and as expected, the internet was a rabbit hole of worst-case scenarios. Every search result seemed more terrifying than the last.

"Stop reading that," I finally said, snatching her phone away.

"I know," She admitted, "But I can't help it."

That night was one of the worst we'd experienced. Neither of us could eat, let alone sleep. The silence between us was heavy, filled with questions we didn't have answers to.

"Do you think... something's really wrong?" Purvi asked quietly in the middle of the night.

I turned to her, struggling to keep my voice steady. "No. We'll talk to our doctor tomorrow. She'll clear everything up."

The next morning, we met our regular doctor, who had just returned from out of town. We explained everything, from the scans to the doctor's casual remark and our sleepless night.

She listened patiently and then smiled. "I understand why you're worried, but let me reassure you—this is normal. The anomaly scan is detailed, and sometimes not all parts are visible due to the baby's position. There's nothing alarming in what you've told me."

Her words were like a balm to our frayed nerves. Purvi let out a sigh of relief, and I felt a weight lift off my chest.

"Thank you, doctor," I said. "We were so scared."

"It's natural," she replied kindly. "But trust me, everything is fine. You're doing great, both of you."

As we left the clinic, I looked at Purvi. "Told you."

She smiled, the first genuine smile I'd seen in 24 hours. "I'm just glad the baby's okay."

We went home, exhausted but finally at peace. That day taught us an important lesson: sometimes, you just need to wait for clarity instead of jumping to conclusions. And more importantly, never trust Doctor Google.

But life didn't stop for us to catch our breath. There were still many pending tasks that needed to be completed before the big day. The paintwork, furniture, and light fittings were all at the finishing stage. Thankfully, these were progressing steadily, and we were confident they would be completed on time. But the Mandir work—that was an entirely different story.

The Mandir idea came to us at the last moment, a sudden inspiration that struck one evening as we discussed how to add a touch of spirituality to our new home. It felt essential to create a dedicated space for peace and prayer, but it left us with a significant challenge: very little time to execute it.

"We'll figure it out," Mom told me confidently. "We just need the right artist."

We wasted no time putting the plan into action. After some research and a few calls, we hired a painter who specialized in religious murals. Our vision was clear: a stunning *Shreenathji* mural that would be the centerpiece of our Mandir, giving it a surreal and divine look.

The painter assured us the work could be completed within ten days. "Don't worry, sir. I've done this before," he said with an air of confidence.

However, things didn't go as planned. For the first three days, the painter didn't even show up. Each time we called, he had an excuse ready.

"Sorry, sir. My bike broke down."
"The materials are delayed."
"I had a family emergency."

I was getting frustrated. "At this rate, we'll have everything ready except the Mandir," Mom said, pacing the room.

"I'll talk to him," I said, trying to stay calm.

When I called the painter again, I was firm but polite. "Look, we're on a tight schedule. We trusted you with this project, but we can't afford any more delays."

He apologized and promised to start the next day. True to his word this time, he finally arrived.

Watching him work was fascinating. Each brushstroke was deliberate, as if he were pouring his devotion into the art. But the delays didn't stop. He would come for a day or two and then disappear for personal reasons.

Mom sighed one evening. "Do you think we should hire someone else?"

"We're too far along to start over," Dad replied. "Let's give him a bit more time. It's frustrating, but I believe he'll deliver."

And deliver he did. Though the work stretched over 15 days instead of the promised 10, the end result was breathtaking. The mural was a masterpiece, with intricate details and vibrant colours that brought Shreenathji to life. The serene expression on the deity's face seemed to radiate peace and divinity.

When the painter unveiled the completed mural, our eyes lit up. "It's beautiful," Purvi whispered, her voice filled with awe.

"All the delays were worth it," Dad said, smiling. "This is exactly what we envisioned," Mom said.

The painter beamed with pride. "Thank you, sir, ma'am. I'm glad you like it."

With the mural completed, we could finally focus on the final preparations for the Vastu Puja and Grah-Pravesh ceremony. The guest list was finalized, and the food menu was carefully planned to include everyone's favourites.

"I've informed everyone coming from outstation, but let's remind them once more," Mom said as she double-checked her list.

Dad made the calls while she sorted through the decorations. "Hello Jai Shree Krishna, just confirming your arrival on the 15th... Yes, the ceremony starts at 10 AM, followed by lunch... Great, see you then!"

The responses were overwhelmingly positive. Everyone was excited to see the new house and celebrate with us.

As the big day approached, we took a moment to stand in the Mandir, admiring the mural. "This house already feels like a home," Purvi said softly, placing her hand on her baby bump.

"It's because of all the love and effort we've poured into it," Mom replied.

She nodded, her eyes glistening with emotion. "I can't wait to start living here."

The next few days were a whirlwind of activity. The furniture was arranged, the lights installed, and the house cleaned from top to bottom. Each corner of the house felt like it had a story to tell, a piece of us woven into it.

"I told you, everything will be fine and completed on time, God is with us, he will take care of everything," Mom said with a smile, echoing the sentiment we had clung to throughout the process.

SIXTH MONTH

The First Kick

The much-awaited day of our new home's

Vastu Puja and housewarming ceremony finally arrived, marking the culmination of months of effort, planning, and anticipation. Most of our outstation guests had already arrived the previous day, bringing with them the warmth of family and the excitement of the occasion. A few more were expected early in the morning, and we had ensured comfortable arrangements for everyone. Fortunately, a nearby house was vacant during this period, allowing us to host our guests without hassle.

The day started early, with a mix of excitement and nervousness in the air. As the first rays of the sun kissed the walls of our new home, the Panditji arrived to begin the preparations for the pooja. Purvi, being eight months pregnant, was not participating in the rituals, as per the traditional belief that pregnant women should avoid certain ceremonies. She stayed with her family and other guests in the nearby house and was going to join us once the pooja was completed.

By 9 AM, the pooja began. The rhythmic chants of the mantras filled the house, creating an aura of peace and divinity. Sitting in front of the sacred fire, I couldn't help but feel a surge of pride and gratitude. This wasn't just a house—it was the manifestation of our dreams, struggles, and countless memories.

As the rituals continued in one corner of the living room, guests wandered through the house, exploring every nook and cranny.

"This is stunning," my uncle exclaimed as he admired the Shreenathji mural in the Mandir. "Whoever did this have outdone themselves."

"It took a while," I said with a smile. "The artist tested our patience, but the result was worth it."

Another guest stopped by the balcony. "The view from here is fantastic! You've chosen such a perfect spot."

"Yes," I replied. "This balcony was one of the reasons we fell in love with this plot."

The pooja concluded by noon, and panditji declared the rituals a success. As he tied a sacred thread around our wrists, he blessed our family and the house, wishing it always be filled with prosperity and happiness.

It was time for lunch, and Chirag, Purvi's brother, had already taken her meal to her room since she couldn't join us. It was important for her to stick to her diet. We had planned an elaborate spread, and although the caterers had promised timely delivery, there were some unexpected delays. The summer heat made the wait feel even longer, but we had arranged for chilled *chaach* (buttermilk) to keep everyone cool.

"This chaach is amazing," one of the guests commented. "Perfect for this weather."

Dad couldn't help but chuckle. "Yes, please have some more. Lunch is also almost ready."

When lunch finally arrived, it wasn't quite up to the mark. The flavours were not as we had hoped, and while some guests were polite about it, a few couldn't hide their disappointment.

After the Pooja, Purvi joined us, her smile lighting up the room. The guests were eager to meet her—some hadn't seen her since the pregnancy news broke. She moved gracefully from one group to another, responding patiently to the usual flood of questions.

"So, any cravings?" someone asked playfully.

"Nothing so far," she replied with a soft laugh.

"But you're glowing!" Manju Aunty chimed in, placing a gentle hand on her arm.

"Thank you," Purvi said, touched by the compliment.

Naresh Uncle came over with his trademark warm smile. "Congratulations on the house, beta."

"Thank you, Uncle," she responded sincerely.

She later took her family on a small tour of the house, proudly showing them the rooms, the Mandir wall, and every little corner.

"This wall," she said, pointing to a corner of the living room, "was where we had planned a completely different design. But then we found this pattern and fell in love with it."

Her brother nodded approvingly. "It's unique and suits the room perfectly."

As the day progressed, we began bidding farewell to the guests. Each departure came with blessings and compliments.

"Your house is so lovely and spacious," an elderly aunt said, holding Mom's hand.

"Thank you," She replied earnestly. "We're grateful for your presence today."

By evening, the house was quiet again, save for the lingering warmth of the day's events. According to tradition, the house shouldn't be left empty after a Vastu Puja, so someone had to stay overnight. Since we hadn't fully moved in yet and there were still some arrangements left to be completed, Purvi and I decided to return to our old home for now. My parents volunteered to stay at the new house for the next couple of nights.

"Are you sure you'll be comfortable here?" I asked my mother as we set up their temporary sleeping arrangements.

She smiled. "Of course. You two need some rest. Go home and relax."

As we rode back to our old house, Purvi leaned her head against me. "It's strange, isn't it?" she said softly.

"What is?" I asked.

"Leaving our new home after everything today."

I nodded, understanding her sentiment. "We'll move in properly soon."

That night, as we lay in bed, exhaustion mixed with contentment. The day hadn't been perfect, but it had been ours—filled with moments of joy, challenges, and memories that would stay with us forever.

Suddenly, Purvi whispered, "Aman!"

"What happened?!" I sat up, startled.

"Quick, give me your hand," she said, grabbing it and placing it gently on her belly. "Feel this?"

I waited, holding my breath.

"I don't feel anything, what happened?" I asked curiously after waiting patiently for few seconds

"Baby kicked, Aman!" she said, her eyes wide and brimming with emotion.

"What? Really? This is the first time, right?" I beamed with excitement.

"Yeah... kind of. I had felt some light movements before, but this—this was different. Stronger. It was definitely a kick." Her voice cracked slightly, a few tears slipping down her cheeks. "Aman, can you believe it? Our baby is kicking now. I felt the first real kick. You have no idea... that feeling.

Purvi continued, her voice softened, "*You are already my everything and everything I have is yours. I* just... I can't wait to see those little feet, those tiny hands, those magical eyes... and that perfect smile. *Waiting for the baby is the hardest and most beautiful part of women's life.*"

I sat there ignoring her words, my hand still resting gently on her belly.

"All is well... All is well... All is well" I murmured, half-laughing, half-serious.

"What are you doing?" she asked, raising an eyebrow. "This isn't a movie, and you're *not* Aamir Khan. The baby's not going to kick on 'All is Well'".

"Worth a try," I said with a grin.

She rolled her eyes, but her smile lingered.

And with that thought, we drifted off to sleep dreaming of those tiny unborn feet and the new chapter that waited for us in our soon-to-be home.

Deciding when to shift to our new home turned out to be more challenging than we anticipated. It wasn't just about moving belongings; it was about moving our hearts, and that wasn't easy. As excited as we were to start living in our new house, the comfort and memories of our old home held us back. It became a bittersweet tug-of-war, each side equally compelling.

For a few days, we found ourselves oscillating between the two places. My parents would stay at the new home at night, ensuring it wasn't left empty, while Purvi and I continued to return to our old home. It felt like we were living two lives—one rooted in the familiarity of the past and the other inching toward the promise of a new beginning.

Priya, my sister, who went back to Mumbai kept nudging us to move to new house. She said unless you don't move into the new house you won't be able to settle properly. And she had a point.

Later that night, back at the old house, Purvi and I sat down to talk. The air was filled with unspoken emotions.

"Priya di is right. Do you think we're hesitating because we're scared?" she asked, her voice barely above a whisper.

I thought about it for a moment. "Maybe. It's not just about leaving this place. It's about leaving the memories, the comfort. Starting something new always comes with a bit of fear."

She nodded, her hand resting on her belly. "But we need to move someday, right, I want to live in new house?"

I looked at her. "Hmm. ok"

The next morning, we took what felt like a monumental step. Unhinging the TV from the wall, a task that should have been mundane, turned into a symbolic act. As I carried the TV to the car, Mom stood by, watching with a mix of emotions.

"Are we really shifting to new house? Are you sure?" she said, her voice tinged with both excitement and nostalgia.

"Yes," I replied, setting the TV down carefully. "This is our way of officially saying goodbye to the old and hello to the new."

Once the TV was set up in the new house, it felt like a declaration. The empty space it left in the old living room seemed to echo the finality of our decision.

That evening, as we sat in the new house watching a show, "It feels different, but it feels right," Purvi whispered.

Surely, it was emotional. Moving out of a place you've called home for most of your life is never easy. *A house is not just a structure; it's an ocean of memories, a silent witness to your journey, and a space filled with countless 'firsts'.* It's the place where you were born, where you took your first steps, and where you had your first falls. Each corner tells a story, and each piece of furniture, no matter how ordinary, holds a special attachment.

Even the smallest, most trivial items—an old, chipped mug or a broken bucket that somehow found its way into a corner of the house—suddenly seem irreplaceable when it's time to leave. It's strange how these insignificant things acquire meaning when they're tied to a place you're leaving behind.

Even though we had moved to the new house, we still came to the old one to pack up the remaining things, gradually shifting everything over.

I sat on the staircase of our old home, running my hand along the banister that I had slid down countless times as a child. "I'm going to miss this," I murmured to Purvi, who stood in the doorway, watching me.

She smiled gently, but I could tell she understood. There was a quiet sadness in the air, one that wasn't just about leaving a house—it was about leaving a piece of us behind.

Just then, Dad walked into the room, his footsteps slow and measured. He stopped by the door, looking around. "This room seems much bigger now," he said, his voice distant. He paused, then added, "But empty."

I nodded, trying to absorb his words. The memories came rushing back—lazy summer afternoons spent playing board games on the living room floor, stormy nights when we huddled together during power cuts, and the aroma of Mom's cooking spreading through the house. It was all there, etched into the walls, the floors, and the air itself.

As we began packing, I realized how much of the house had been tied to our daily rhythms. The creak of the front door was like a familiar greeting, the squeaky window in my childhood room a small annoyance I had learned to love, and the kitchen's tiled floor still bore faint scratches from the time I dropped a heavy skillet as a teenager.

"This house has seen everything Purvi... Do you think we'll feel the same about the new house?" I asked.

"It'll take time," Purvi admitted. "But eventually, yes. We'll make new memories there. And one day, maybe, we'll sit and reminisce about that house too."

"Ouch!" Purvi exclaimed, pressing a hand gently against her belly.

"Kick again?" I asked, quickly moving closer and placing my hand over hers.

"Nothing yet," I said after a few seconds of silence.

"Wait..." she whispered, grabbing my hand and holding it still.

Thump. There it was.

My eyes lit up. "Yes! Yes, I felt something—it's like a little knock from the inside. Wow!"

She smiled, her face glowing. "Yes... that's a kick."

In those moments I forgot about everything... and was just lost in that knock from our little one. It was the moment when I could feel its existence, from baby bump... it became baby, so real... so soon... with just one kick.

My parents were having their own moment of reflection. My mother stood in the balcony, her fingers trailing over the rose bushes she had planted years ago. "These roses have seen so much," she said softly. "They've bloomed every year, no matter what."

Dad was in the living room, flipping through an old photo album. "This is where we started," he said, holding up a picture of him and mom standing in the freshly painted living room, decades younger. "It wasn't perfect, but it was ours."

The decision to leave wasn't made lightly. For days, we wrestled with the emotional weight of it. The house was more than bricks and mortar; it was a part of us.

When the final day came, the air was heavy with emotions. The movers had already taken most of our belongings to the new house, but there were still a few last things to gather. I stood in my childhood room, now empty, and felt a lump rise in my throat.

"This room... these walls...." I said aloud. Purvi came up behind me, resting a hand on my shoulder. "It's okay to feel this way. It just means this place meant a lot to you."

We gathered as a family in the living room one last time. My mom lit a diya, placing it on the windowsill. "For good energy," she explained. "And for gratitude."

We drove to the new house in near silence, each of us lost in our thoughts. When we arrived, the new house felt foreign. But as we unpacked and began arranging things, a sense of excitement crept in.

That evening, as we sat in the living room of our new home, surrounded by half-unpacked boxes, Purvi nudged me. "I really like it here and I think the baby will too. I can already imagine us sitting here years from now, talking about all the memories we're going to make."

I smiled. "Yeah. It's the start of something new."

And in that moment, I realized she was right. A house becomes a home through the people and the memories you create together. While the old house would always hold a special place in our hearts, the new one was waiting to be filled with stories of its own.

Now, we had finally moved into our new home. It was a milestone we had long anticipated, but the reality of settling into a completely new space wasn't as effortless as we had imagined. The first few days were a whirlwind of adjustments— finding our way around, organizing the essentials, and trying to make the unfamiliar feel like home.

Purvi, being in an advanced stage of pregnancy, needed all the comfort and care we could provide. I remember her sitting on the new couch, her hands resting gently on her baby bump, looking around with a mix of excitement and apprehension.

"This place feels so big," she said one evening as we unpacked yet another box. "I mean, it's beautiful, but it's going to take time to feel like home."

I smiled, pausing my work. "That's okay, we have all the time. You just focus on resting and taking care of yourself."

We had made her comfort a top priority. The bedroom was the first space we completely set up, ensuring she had a cozy and peaceful retreat. "Do you like the arrangement?" I asked after setting up the bed with her favorite soft, floral-patterned bedsheets.

She nodded, giving me a small smile. "It's perfect. Thank you."

But as settled as we tried to feel, there was still the excitement—and stress—of what lay ahead. The next big thing on our to-do list: the Angarni, Gujarati baby shower. The planning had begun, and the weight of tradition, family expectations, and the joy of welcoming our little one all seemed to come together at once.

SEVENTH MONTH

Baby Shower

In our Gujarati tradition, the baby shower, or

Angarni, is not just a ceremony; it's a celebration of life, culture, and blessings for the unborn child and the mother. It's a grand affair that spans three to five days, filled with rituals, food, music, dance, and laughter. Purvi's Angarni was no different—if anything, it was even more vibrant and memorable.

The preparations began weeks in advance. Invitations were sent out, decorations were finalized, and endless discussions over the menu and outfits filled the house.

Mom was especially nervous. The Angarni (*Seemant Ceremony*) is considered a deeply auspicious ceremony—a chance to seek blessings from Mataji (*Randal Devi*)—and she knew how important it was to get everything just right. None of us had any prior experience organizing such an event, so the responsibility of planning and executing it fell almost entirely on her shoulders. She was anxious, yes, and visibly exhausted at times, but still, she carried on—holding everything together, managing every detail, and making sure everyone felt included and involved.

Purvi's sister Ruchi arrived a few days prior to help with the preparations and spend some quality time with Purvi. Her arrival brought a wave of relief to both of us, but especially to Purvi, whose energy had started to dip as the due date neared. Ruchi's infectious energy and endless supply of jokes filled the house with laughter.

One evening, the two of them were going through outfits in the bedroom when Purvi held up a vibrant red and green lehenga.

"Do you think I'll look okay in this?" she asked, eyeing herself in the mirror.

"The lehenga? Yes!" Ruchi said, squinting. "But those earrings? Absolutely not."

"But... I don't have any others. I thought these matched," Purvi replied, sounding a little defeated.

Ruchi rolled her eyes playfully. "You *thought* these matched? Oh, Jiji..."

She searched through her bag and pulled out a small pouch. "Don't worry... I came prepared."

Purvi's eyes lit up as Ruchi opened the pouch, revealing a beautiful collection of earrings. "Oh my god, you bought so many! And they're all so pretty!"

"Try this pair," Ruchi said, handing her one with a delicate gold and green design.

Purvi clipped them on and turned toward the mirror.

"Yes!" Ruchi clapped. "Perfect match. And you're welcome."

Purvi smiled wide, the kind that came from feeling seen and cared for. "Thank you, Ruchi."

The first day of the celebrations was a modest gathering with close family. It began with *Grah shanti*, a puja to ensure the well-being of the mother and baby. The priest chanted mantras as Purvi sat, her hands folded and eyes closed, a serene smile on her face.

My mother leaned in and whispered, "Did you check with the caterers? Make sure they're preparing the prasad separately and have it ready on time."

"Yes, Mummy," I reassured her. "Don't worry—everything's going smoothly."

She nodded slowly. "I hope so..."

Priya, who had taken full charge of the decorations, beamed with pride as she showed off the vibrant rangoli designs at the entrance and the marigold garlands hanging across the doorway. The scent of fresh flowers mixed with incense lingered in the air, wrapping the house in a festive charm.

Wiping sweat from her forehead, she turned to me and said, "This heat is killing me. But just look at this—totally worth it, right?"

I nodded, impressed. "It looks beautiful. But wait... why aren't you ready yet?" I said looking at her.

She rolled her eyes. "I was *just* about to get ready."

"Well, hurry up! Mummy had already reminded you twice. And trust me, you do *not* want to be on her hit list right now. She's juggling a hundred things."

Priya groaned dramatically, already halfway up the stairs. "Fine, fine! I'm going."

I chuckled as she disappeared, as I turned, I noticed the caterer signalling me from across the hall.

I walked over to him. "Lunch is almost ready. Shall we start serving?" he asked.

"Great! Yes, please prepare the tables. I'll invite everyone," I replied.

I turned to my cousins, Prem and Pratik. "Let's call everyone for lunch!" I asked.

"Sure," Prem said, nodding.

They moved towards the group of guests who were sitting and chatting. First, they approached the eldest members—Dada and our uncles.

"Dada, Bharat Uncle, please come. Lunch is served," Prem called out.

"Santhosh Uncle, Sunil Uncle, Rajat Bhaiya, come, let's eat," Pratik announced.

Finally, Prem turned to the ladies.

"Ridhima, call all the ladies for lunch," he said.

Ridhima nodded and went to gather the women.

Soon, everyone gathered around the lunch tables and began enjoying the meal.

"This aamras is *too* delicious!" exclaimed Sonali Didi, savouring each bite.

"Yes, everything tastes so good. It's like I'm having a proper home-cooked meal after ages," added Roopali Didi, clearly impressed.

The aroma, the flavours, the chatter—it all came together perfectly. Gradually, conversations shifted from the scorching heat to delicious food. The lunch had turned into a warm, shared celebration in itself.

The pooja had gone smoothly too, and with satisfied smiles and full plates, it was clear everyone was genuinely happy.

The second day was all about gifts and blessings, *Khodo Bharavo* (Literal meaning is to fill the mother to be's lap with wholeness & abundance). In our tradition, we believe in showering the mother-to-be with blessings and gifts. Relatives and friends poured with beautiful gifts and blessings.

One by one, relatives approached Purvi, handing her items ranging from gold jewellery to handwoven blankets, all while offering their heartfelt blessings. Her hands were soon overflowing with gifts, and her face was a mix of gratitude and mild embarrassment.

Ruchi and her cousins had beautifully decorated a toy train—each tiny compartment filled with gifts, sweets, baby clothes, and little surprises. It looked straight out of a dream, carefully crafted with love.

"Wow, this is so heartwarming and beautiful," Purvi said, her eyes wide with wonder. "You did *all* of this in just one day?"

"Yes," Ruchi grinned, "but it wouldn't have been possible without Sonali Didi's help."

"Thank you so much, Didi. This is such a lovely gift," Purvi said, her voice full of gratitude.

Sonali Didi walked over with a warm smile and gently pinched Purvi's cheek. "Beta, it's all for the baby. Enjoy your day"

Apart from all the joyful celebrations, there was one more special ritual everyone had been looking forward to. It's a sweet custom where the *Devar*—the younger brother-in-law—gently applies *kankoo* (kumkum) across the cheeks of the *mom-to-be*. It's his playful way of reminding her, *"Don't forget about me now that you're going to have a baby!"*

As Pratik stepped forward with a mischievous grin, he dipped his fingers in the red *kankoo* and said teasingly, *"Bhabhi*, don't worry, I'll just put a tiny bit!"

Purvi laughed, holding up her hand in mock protest. *"Pratik bhai*, I still have to click so many pictures, put very little ok!"

Everyone around chuckled, and the moment turned into a mix of laughter, love, and the kind of memories that last a lifetime.

After the rituals, it was time for the feast. The spread was lavish, featuring traditional Gujarati delicacies like *undhiyu, khaman, dhokla*, and *jalebi*. Guests indulged happily, praising the arrangements.

"This *kadhi* is amazing!" one relative exclaimed. "Caterers did a terrific job!"

I glanced at Purvi, who was nibbling on a piece of *puran poli*. "Is it up to your standards?" I teased.

"It's perfect," she said with a content sigh. "Though I think I'm going to need a nap after this."

The evening brought a new level of energy as Purvi's sisters took the reins of the get-together. I handed over the event to them entirely, trusting their ability to make it memorable. Deepali didi, Purvi's cousin sister, proved herself to be a pro at anchoring the evening's festivities, keeping the energy high. Dance performances by Priya, Ruchi, and our cousins were a hit. The whole family danced and sang, their laughter echoing through the evening. Purvi sat at the edge of the makeshift dance floor, clapping along and occasionally getting pulled up by relatives to sway gently.

"Take it slow!" I called out, laughing as one of her cousins dragged her into the circle.

"I'm fine!" she replied, her face lit up with joy. It was beautiful to see her so happy, surrounded by so much love.

The crowd was so energized that the evening turned into a mini celebration of its own. Deepali didi took the mic and joked, "Okay, now coming with her terrific moves. Priya, you're up next!"

Priya lit up the room with her signature performance on *Kajra Re*, her expressions as lively as ever. Then came the most touching part of the evening—Ruchi and Chirag took the stage with an emotional performance. A soft, heartfelt song played as they danced with grace and deep emotion, joined halfway by their cousins.

Everyone cheered, and the night was filled with lively performances, spontaneous dances, and plenty of laughter.

The third day was the most significant: the *Angarni* itself. The venue was transformed into a festive haven, with marigold garlands and *rangoli* designs adorning every corner. A grand swing (*jhoola*) was set up, decorated with flowers. Purvi, dressed in her lehenga, was seated on it, looking every bit the glowing mother-to-be.

As part of the ritual, the women of the family took turns rocking the swing gently while singing traditional songs. The melodies filled the air, creating an atmosphere of warmth and togetherness.

Purvi looked absolutely stunning—radiant and glowing in her red and green Banarasi saree. But what truly stole the show was her floral jewellery and that intricately styled bun, all crafted with real flowers lovingly prepared by my mom. The highlight was the peacock-style floral bun—it was nothing short of a work of art.

"Mummy, you were right," I said, admiring Purvi from a distance. "Using real flowers was the perfect choice. She looks gorgeous, especially with that bun. It's so unique."

My mom beamed with pride. "Yes, many people have been complimenting it too. I told you I'm always right! You really should listen to me more often."

We both laughed, but deep down, I was grateful—for her touch, her efforts, and the way she made the day even more special.

At one point, Purvi leaned over to me and whispered, "This feels surreal. I feel so special."

I smiled and whispered back, "It's your moment. Enjoy every bit of it."

Once most of the guests had arrived and showered their blessings on Purvi, our photographer gave us a subtle signal—it was time to sneak away for a quick photo session. We were exhausted by then, but no way were we going to let that stop us from capturing some lifelong memories.

With smiles still intact and a bit of playful energy left, we posed in a few candid shots, recreated some of our favourite Instagram-saved poses, and clicked a bunch with our families too. Despite the heat and the fatigue, those few moments felt light, fun, and beautifully real—something we knew we'd look back on fondly for years to come.

The *Angarni* wasn't just an event; it was an experience that brought everyone closer together. It was a celebration of love, family, and the anticipation of new life. As the last of the guests departed, we felt a deep sense of gratitude—for the blessings, the memories, and the joy that filled those five unforgettable days.

After the grand *Shrimant Ceremony (Angarni)*, we bid farewell to our guests, each one offering warm blessings and heartfelt congratulations. The surrounding that had just been buzzing with laughter, music, and celebration slowly returned to calm. We were left with warm memories and tired smiles.

Back in our new home, we all fell onto the couches, utterly exhausted but equally content.

EIGHT MONTH

The Preparations Begins

Adjusting to our new house wasn't as seamless as we had hoped. It was no surprise that we faced difficulties, given how attached we were to the old house. Everything there, though chaotic and cluttered, was organized in a way that suited our needs. Each corner held familiarity, and even the mess had a certain charm. Most importantly, we had the luxury of maids who handled almost everything—cooking, cleaning, washing—which had made life much easier. Here, however, we found ourselves starting from scratch.

"We need to get things from the old house," she added, a hint of nostalgia in her voice.

"True," I nodded, glancing around the spotless new counters. "And also, let's make a list of what new items we need to buy."

"That's Purvi's department," Mom said with a smile.

"Already on it, Mummy," Purvi chimed in from the dining table, her phone open with a running list of essentials.

"Great. Then let's plan a D-Mart run this weekend," I suggested.

"But first," Mom said, while cooking, "let's go to the old house and bring back some of the must-haves."

While we moved from room to room packing the essentials, bits of the past seemed to fall into our hands.

"Remember this toy car?" Mom held up a dusty red plastic car with faded stickers. "You used to roam around the entire house with this!"

I chuckled, taking it from her. "Yeah, but it doesn't even work now."

"It's not that bad," she insisted. "Your kid will love it. These things aren't just toys, they're legacy."

She moved to a cupboard and pulled out a pristine, unused dinner set.

"And look at this—this set is beautiful. No way we're leaving it behind."

"But Mummy," I smiled, "you've never used it, and I honestly doubt you will. It'll just end up in storage again."

"I will," she said with quiet pride. "I was saving all of this for the new house. Now, I finally have a reason to use it."

I looked at her, shaking my head with a grin. "Fine. There's no winning with you."

She smiled back, victorious.

Box by box, we carefully gathered utensils, cleaning supplies, and a few sentimental items that held more memories than purpose. *Too bad we can only pack the things... not the memories.*

With the car packed full, we left the familiar corners of our old home and drove back to the new one.

Back at the new house, the first order of business was finding help for the daily chores. With Purvi's pregnancy and the sheer workload, we knew we couldn't manage everything on our own.

"Should we ask the neighbours?" Purvi suggested as we sipped tea later that afternoon.

"Good idea," I said. "Let's start with Mrs. Mehta next door. She seems friendly."

We knocked on her door, and she greeted us warmly. After a few pleasantries, we explained our situation.

"Oh, don't worry," she said with a reassuring smile. "I'll give you the numbers of a few maids who work in this colony. They're reliable."

To our surprise, it didn't take much effort to find a maid. By the end of the day, we had hired someone for cleaning and washing.

"Thank goodness for that," Purvi said, visibly relieved. "Now we can focus on baby's preparations."

"See? One step at a time," I said, patting her shoulder.

The journey of adjusting to our new house had just begun, but with each task accomplished, it started feeling a little more like home. The small victories—like hiring a maid—became reasons to celebrate.

As it was peak summer heat was relentless, and it was becoming increasingly difficult for us to cope with the sweltering temperatures. Being pregnant, she was already enduring enough discomfort, and the added warmth only made things worse. Every day seemed more unbearable than the last, and it became clear we had to find a solution.

One evening, as we sat in the living room with the ceiling fan working overtime, I sighed, "I don't think I can handle another day like this."

Purvi nodded in agreement. "You're right."

"It's time to invest in an AC. It's long overdue now." I continued.

"Yes, let's get one for your room," Dad said.

The decision was made, but as with every big purchase, it came with its own set of dilemmas. We dived into research mode, browsing online reviews and asking friends for recommendations.

"Okay, so what's more important—energy efficiency or cooling speed?" I asked, staring at a comparison chart on my phone.

Over a quick call, Priya chimed in, "Both! We can't afford to compromise on either, especially with these temperatures. Check if they have inverter technology. It's supposed to save energy."

After narrowing down our options, we were stuck between two popular brands—Panasonic and Samsung. Both had glowing reviews and similar features.

"I think Panasonic is the better choice," I suggested. "Its reviews mention quieter performance, which is perfect for nights."

"But Samsung has a slightly lower price online," Purvi countered. "Should we consider that?"

"And here's the million-dollar question," I added with a chuckle. "Do we buy it online or visit a store?"

To settle the debate, we decided to visit a familiar electronics store that had served us well in the past. As we entered, the cool air-conditioned interior felt like a slice of heaven.

The salesperson greeted us with a smile. "Looking for an air conditioner? Let me help you."

After explaining our requirements, he quickly recommended the Panasonic model. "It's reliable, energy-efficient, and we can match the online price for you," he assured us.

Dad looked at me, eyebrows raised. "That's a win-win, right?"

"Absolutely," I replied. "Let's go for it. Can we have it installed today?" I asked the salesperson.

He nodded. "Sure thing. We'll have a technician at your home in a few hours."

True to their promise, the installation was done by evening. As the AC hummed to life, the cool air filled the room, and for the first time in days, we felt genuine relief.

That night, we set the temperature to a comfortable 24°C, a drastic contrast to the scorching 45°C outside. Lying in bed, Purvi said softly, "This... This feels so good, so glad we took this decision."

"Agreed, it was much needed." I responded.

The eighth month of Purvi's pregnancy marked an exciting milestone—our long-awaited pregnancy photoshoot. It was something we had both been looking forward to for weeks.

We already had saved and shared so many posts and reels from Instagram to each other, regarding different ideas, dress, looks and specially poses. So, when the day was finally getting closer, we couldn't contain our excitement and began preparing.

From Amazon, we ordered a variety of dresses, props, and accessories—everything from delicate flower crowns to playful signs with captions like "*Mom-to-be*" and "*Little one loading...*".

"I hope these props look good in pictures," Purvi said, inspecting them when they arrived.

"They will," I reassured her, holding up a black dress she'd chosen for the shoot. "This one will look best in photos."

I decided against hiring a professional photographer. "I can handle the camera," I said confidently. "After all, I've taken a million pictures on our vacations."

Purvi smirked. "Yes, but this isn't just a sunset or a plate of food. These are *my pregnancy pictures!*"

"You're doubting my abilities, Madam?" I said dramatically. "Just wait and watch."

The big day finally arrived. We cleared the living room, shifted the furniture, laid out a few props, and let the morning sunlight pour in through the windows. The natural light cast a soft, golden glow—perfect for what we had in mind.

Purvi got ready on her own—doing her hair and makeup with calm focus, but it was her natural pregnancy glow that truly made her shine. She looked beautiful, effortlessly.

"Okay, first outfit—black dress," I said, lifting the camera and giving her an encouraging smile. "Let's start with a classic look."

"Now make a heart over your belly," I guided, as she smiled and posed. Click.

We moved from one pose to another, slowly ticking off the shots we'd planned, pausing often to laugh at the awkward ones or redo the good ones that didn't turn out quite right.

"I'm already tired," Purvi said, flopping onto the couch for a moment.

"We've just started!" I teased. "Okay, okay, I'll be quick. Let's change into the jumpsuit now."

The jumpsuit brought a fun, playful vibe to the shoot. We added props—tiny shoes, a baby sign, and one of those chalkboards that read "Coming Soon." I realized then that clicking the perfect photo was harder than it looked—finding the right angle, the right moment, and the right smile all at once was no easy task.

"Does this sign look straight?" Purvi asked, holding it up.

I adjusted it slightly. "Now it does. Hold that pose—perfect!"

We were nearly done with Purvi's solo shots, but the couple photos were still pending. I tried a few selfies, switching between the front and rear cameras, but nothing seemed to match the quality of the earlier shots. My patience was wearing thin.

Just then, Mom walked in, carrying a tray of water. "Aren't you done yet? Wow, Purvi—you look absolutely gorgeous!"

"Thank you, Mummy. No, not done yet. Our couple clicks aren't turning out good," Purvi said, a little disappointed.

"Mummy! You can click us," I said, half-joking, half-serious.

"Me?" she blinked.

"Yes! I'll set the camera settings and the angle. You just have to press the button." I smiled, hopeful.

"Okay, let's try," she said with a shrug.

With Mom's help, the process suddenly felt smoother. She adjusted the props, fixed Purvi's hair mid-shoot, and even suggested some candid, sweet poses we hadn't thought of. And to our surprise—she nailed the angles.

"Wow, Mummy, those are really good clicks!" Purvi said, genuinely impressed as we flipped through the shots.

"I told you!" Mom said, with a victorious grin.

After hours of shooting, we finally wrapped up. The room was a mess, but the memory of the day made it all worth it. "You did well," Purvi said, looking at the preview of the photos on the camera.

"Thanks, but my work isn't done yet," I replied. "Now I have to sort and edit these."

Over the next few hours, I meticulously went through the photos, choosing the best ones and editing them to perfection. The final results were stunning—Purvi glowing in every frame, her joy and excitement practically radiating through the pictures.

When I showed her the edited photos, her face lit up. "These are amazing!" she exclaimed. "I can't believe you did this!"

"See? Told you we don't need professional help," I said with a grin.

However, when it came time to upload them to Instagram, Purvi hesitated. "I'm not sure," she said, biting her lip. "What if people's *nazar* ruins everything?"

"You don't have to share them publicly," I said. "We can keep them for ourselves or share them with close family."

She nodded. "Let's do that for now. I'll send them to my family and relatives. Instagram can wait."

Purvi shared them with her family and was receiving lots of compliments, that evening, we sat together, scrolling through the photos on my laptop. Each picture told a story—a moment frozen in time, capturing the anticipation and excitement of welcoming our baby.

"Do you ever think about how our life has changed?" Purvi asked one evening, her voice soft as she leaned into the couch. "Just a year ago we were casually watching Netflix or planning a spontaneous trip."

"Yeah... I do," I replied, smiling at the memory. "Those carefree days—binge-watching till 3 a.m. and then sleeping till afternoon. *Nowadays, waking up without an alarm feels like a luxury not everyone can afford.*"

She chuckled. "Right! And don't get me wrong—I already love this baby more than anything. But... you do realize that we won't be able to live like that anymore? That live-in-the-moment, no-responsibilities kind of life. Won't you miss it?"

"Ya I mean...," I nodded. "Those were golden days. But here's the thing—I believe *if you're always living the same routine, no matter how fun it seems, you're not lucky... you're just stuck."*

She raised an eyebrow, curious.

"And besides," I continued, "look at what's ahead of us. We have so many platinum days waiting. The baby's first laugh, first step, first word... many other firsts. And this is only the beginning—there will be so many joyful moments, that you'll wish... to live them again and again."

I glanced at her, my voice a little softer.

"Yes, there'll be ups and downs, but *a bumpy ride will always give you stories to share, a little bit of fear, some forgettable tears and lots of moments to cheer... and... that's life.*"

She looked at me for a long second, a small smile tugging at her lips. "You're just... a magician with words. Always know exactly what to say. That's how you trapped me, you know—your charming words."

"Trapped you?" I laughed.

Soon, an anxious moment turned into laughter— light, unexpected, and real.

In our culture, there's a unique tradition that the baby doesn't wear new clothes for the first two to three weeks after birth. Instead, families borrow clothes from relatives or friends who no longer need them. Initially, I found this custom quite odd and even questioned its logic.

One evening, as Purvi and I were preparing for the baby's arrival, I brought it up. "Have you thought about this whole 'no new clothes' thing?" I asked, swapping through reels on my phone.

Purvi looked up from her spot on the bed. "Of course. Mom told me about it."

"But why old clothes?" I asked, my tone genuinely curious. "Wouldn't it be nice to dress the baby in something new and special?"

Purvi smiled knowingly. "It's tradition, and traditions often have practical reasons. Think about it—newborns grow incredibly fast. New clothes might only fit for a week or two, and then they're useless."

"That does make sense," I admitted. "But still, wouldn't it be nice to have at least one new outfit for pictures or something?"

Purvi laughed. "Don't worry. Mom said we can dress the baby in new clothes for the naming ceremony after a few weeks. Until then, we stick to the old ones."

And Purvi's cousin sister, Sonali Didi, who fortunately lived in the same city, had already offered to help. "Don't even think about buying anything! I have everything you'll need for the baby's first month," Sonali di had assured her over a phone call. Her warm, loving tone made Purvi feel instantly at ease.

"Are you sure, Didi? I don't want to trouble you," Purvi said hesitantly, her hand resting protectively on her baby bump.

"Arrey, what trouble? It's all just lying there, and my kids have outgrown it anyway. You must come for lunch this week, and I'll send you home with everything," Sonali replied enthusiastically.

A few days later, Purvi visited Sonali Didi's house for lunch. The aroma of freshly cooked Gujarati delicacies filled the air as soon as she entered. "Welcome, Purvi! Sit, sit! You must be tired," Sonali greeted her, pulling out a chair at the dining table.

Purvi smiled, feeling a sense of warmth and belonging. "I'm fine, Didi. Thank you for inviting me. It's been a while since we've had a proper catch-up."

The lunch spread was nothing short of a feast—soft rotis, sabzi, dal, rice, and a generous helping of Sonali's signature kheer. As they ate, they reminisced about old times, shared laughter, and talked excitedly about the baby.

"Purvi, you're glowing! Motherhood suits you," Sonali remarked, her eyes twinkling.

"Thank you, Didi. It's been a mix of excitement and nervousness," Purvi admitted.

"Don't worry. You'll be a fantastic mom. And remember, I'm always just a call away," Sonali reassured her.

After lunch, Sonali brought out a large bag stuffed with baby essentials. "Here, this has everything you'll need—onesies, langots, caps, inners, napkins, blankets... you name it, it's in here."

Purvi's eyes widened as she peeked inside. "Didi, this is so much! Are you sure I can take all of this?"

"Of course! These were my kids' things, and now it's your turn to use them. It's all in great condition, and you won't have to worry about a thing for the first month," Sonali said, placing a reassuring hand on Purvi's shoulder.

Touched by the gesture, Purvi hugged her tightly. "Thank you, Didi. This means so much to me."

Sonali laughed. "No formalities, okay? Just promise me you'll visit again soon."

Back home, Purvi unpacked the bag and marvelled at the thoughtful selection. Every item felt like a small blessing, filled with love and care. When she showed the clothes to me, I smiled. "Sonali Didi really went all out, didn't she?"

Purvi nodded. "She's always been like that—so giving, so kind. I'm lucky to have her here."

We were ready—not with shiny new clothes, but with a collection of meaningful, love-filled garments that made this tradition truly special.

Everything was going smoothly, and we were settling into the rhythm of expecting our baby. But one evening, something terrifying happened that shook us to the core. Purvi suddenly clutched her chest, her face contorted with pain. "It's burning... it's unbearable," she gasped, collapsing onto the bed.

I rushed to her side, panic rising like a tidal wave. "Purvi! What's happening? Tell me where it hurts!"

She could barely speak through the pain. "It's around my heart... it feels like it's on fire," she managed to say between breaths. My heart was pounding as I tried to comfort her.

I immediately dialled Mom, who was at the shop, sensed the urgency in my voice when I called her. "I'm coming home right now," she said without hesitation.

And the called our gynaecologist, the doctor answered after a few rings. "Doctor, it's urgent! Purvi is in tremendous pain around her chest. She can't even move," I blurted out, my voice trembling.

"Calm down," the doctor replied firmly but kindly. "It sounds like severe acidity. Did she eat anything unusual or have an irregular routine today?"

I thought back to her day. "She didn't sleep well last night and had some extra cups of tea in the afternoon," I said, realizing this might be the culprit.

"That's likely the cause," the doctor confirmed. "Acidity during pregnancy is common, especially in the later months. It can feel intense, but it's not dangerous. I'll prescribe a syrup for her. Give her the proper doses, keep her calm, and she should feel better by night."

Mom arrived just as I was hanging up the call. Her face was lined with worry, but she immediately sprang into action. "Let's follow the doctor's instructions. Where's the prescription?" she asked.

I quickly fetched the syrup from the nearby pharmacy while Mom stayed with Purvi, gently stroking her hair and speaking soothingly. "Don't worry, beta. It's just acidity. You'll feel better soon," she reassured Purvi, who nodded weakly.

Giving Purvi the syrup and ensuring she rested wasn't easy. She was still in significant discomfort, and watching her suffer was agonizing. "Is it getting better?" I asked every half hour, hoping for a positive response.

"It's a little less intense now," Purvi said faintly after a couple of doses. Seeing even a slight improvement was a relief.

As the evening wore on, we discussed her day in detail, trying to piece together what could have triggered the episode. "I told you that extra tea wasn't a good idea," Mom chided gently.

"I know, Mummy," Purvi admitted. "I didn't think it would cause this much trouble."

By late night, the syrup and rest finally started working. Purvi was sitting up, sipping water cautiously. "I'm feeling better now," she said, her voice stronger than before.

I exhaled deeply, realizing I had been holding my breath. "Thank God! You scared me so much," I said, holding her hand tightly.

"I scared myself too," she admitted with a weak smile. "I promise to take better care of my routine from now on. Proper food, no skipping meals, and definitely no extra tea."

Mom, who had been quietly observing, nodded approvingly. "Good, beta. You're carrying a precious life inside you."

Purvi looked at me with determination. "I'll stick to my promise. No more careless mistakes. This baby deserves the best from me."

As we drifted off to sleep, I silently resolved to keep an even closer eye on her health and routine.

After the unsettling incident with her health, we decided to make some lifestyle changes. One of the most significant ones was incorporating regular night walks after dinner. While we had done this occasionally before, we now took it much more seriously. It was no longer just a casual stroll; it became a commitment to better health for Purvi and, indirectly, for me too. We also began including coconut water in her daily routine, just as the doctor had advised.

"Ready for our first official night walk?" Purvi asked me after our dinner one evening. The cool breeze was refreshing, a pleasant contrast to the stuffy indoors.

"Let's do it," I replied with a determined smile, though her movements were slow and deliberate.

We had downloaded a walking app to track our steps, distance, and time. "Okay, setting the timer for 30 minutes," Purvi said, fiddling with my phone. "We'll gradually increase, ok?"

"30 minutes is fine for now," I said, while putting on my slippers.

As we walked through the quiet streets of our neighbourhood, we found ourselves talking about everything and nothing.

Do you remember our Varanasi trip?" Purvi asked, her voice laced with nostalgia.

"How could I forget?" I smiled. "That trip was full of uncertainties. It turned into a proper adventure—nothing went as planned."

She laughed softly. "Yeah... and who would've thought I was already pregnant then?"

"Seriously," I said, shaking my head in disbelief. "It was so unexpected. But now, looking back... it feels like it was meant to be. Being in *Kashi* at that moment, standing in front of *Mahadev*, not knowing what was growing inside you... it was more than just a coincidence."

"You're right," she said quietly, pressing her hands against her belly. "Everything really does happen for a reason. And this—this little miracle—is the best thing that could've ever happened to us."

Back home, as we sipped on warm water, I couldn't help but feel proud. It wasn't just a walk—it was a step toward a healthier routine and a promise to prioritize well-being. Purvi looked more relaxed, and her cheeks had a faint glow. "Thank you for doing this with me," she said softly.

"Like I have a choice," I teased, nudging her gently.

She smiled, resting her hand on her belly.

Those night walks slowly became our little ritual. It wasn't just about staying active anymore—it became our time. In the quiet of those late evenings, under the dim streetlights and a star-studded sky, a space where we could talk freely, dream aloud, laugh at old memories, and imagine the world we were about to build with our baby.

NINTH MONTH

Our Baby

As we stepped into the final month of pregnancy, excitement and anticipation filled the air. The countdown had officially begun, and every passing day brought us closer to meeting our baby. However, with excitement came a mix of nervousness and uncertainty.

During our ninth month check-up, Doctor Mehta smiled reassuringly at us. "You're almost there now," she said. "Just remember, there's no hard and fast rule that the baby must arrive exactly after completing nine months or 40 weeks. Babies have their timelines."

Purvi nodded, though her brow furrowed slightly. "But the Estimated Delivery Date, it's just a guess, right?" she asked.

"Not exactly a guess," Doctor Mehta replied. "The EDD is based on your last period and a standard 40-week cycle. It's an estimate. Babies can arrive a bit earlier or even later. What's most important is monitoring your and the baby's health."

I chimed in, "What are the main things we need to watch for this month?"

"The final month is crucial," Doctor explained. "We monitor frequently to check for complications, such as the baby's heart rate, movement, or, in rare cases, the baby passing meconium (poop) in the womb. These are manageable with proper care, but it's why we recommend visits every 4-5 days."

The frequency of the doctor's appointments was an adjustment for us. "Every 2-3 days?" I exclaimed as we left the clinic.

"Yes, this is common, I have seen on reels" She reassured me.

With every passing day, Purvi's restlessness grew. "I feel like a ticking time bomb," she joked one morning. "Every little cramp or movement makes me wonder, 'Is this it?'"

I chuckled. "You're not alone."

"Do you think the baby will take after you and arrive late?" I teased.

"Or take after you and arrive early to surprise us," She shot back.

One evening, while we were on our nightly walk, Purvi paused to look up at the stars. "I wonder what life will be like once the baby's here," she mused.

"Chaotic, sleepless, and amazing," I replied with a grin.

She laughed, but her eyes welled up, like the first monsoon rain waiting to fall. "I just hope I'm a good mom."

I stopped and turned to her. "Purvi, you're already an incredible mom. The way you've cared for this baby and prepared for their arrival—it's inspiring."

She smiled, wiping her tears.

As we entered the final weeks of Purvi's pregnancy, our weekly visits to the doctor became a cornerstone of our routine. Each appointment carried a blend of relief and anticipation, as we sought assurance that everything was progressing smoothly while grappling with the unknowns of labour and delivery.

On a sunny Wednesday afternoon, we found ourselves seated in Doctor Mehta's clinic. The waiting room buzzed with the hushed murmurs of other expectant couples and the occasional cry of a newborn. When our turn came, Doctor greeted us with her characteristic warm smile.

"So, how are we doing this week?" she asked, pulling up Purvi's file.

"I've been feeling fine," Purvi responded, though a hint of nervousness flickered in her eyes. "No major discomforts, just the usual backache and tiredness."

Doctor nodded, checking Purvi's blood pressure and examining her reports. "Everything seems good," she said reassuringly. "The baby is growing well, and all the vitals are normal."

I decided it was time to ask the question that had been on our minds. "Doctor, is there anything specific we can do to prepare for labour? Like, should Purvi follow a certain diet or do special exercises to increase the chances of a normal delivery?"

Doctor's expression turned serious, yet kind. "Let me explain something," she began. "There's no guaranteed formula for a normal delivery. Whether it's a vaginal birth or a caesarean, the decision is made based on the circumstances at the time of delivery. Right now, everything looks normal, so there's no need to make drastic changes."

Purvi hesitated before asking, "But I've heard that doing daily yoga or walking regularly can help avoid a C-section. Is that true?"

Doctor Mehta smiled knowingly. "That's a common belief, and while staying active is beneficial, it's not a magic solution. I've seen women who do yoga every day still require a caesarean, and others who spend most of their day seated in an office have a smooth normal delivery. Every pregnancy is unique."

"So, what should we focus on?" I asked, wanting to ensure we were doing everything right.

"Stay consistent with what you're already doing," she advised. "Light exercises, daily walks, and a balanced diet are all great. But don't stress about the outcome. The goal is a healthy baby and a healthy mother, regardless of the method."

As we left the clinic, Purvi looked thoughtful. "I guess I was overthinking a bit," she admitted.

"You're doing amazing," I reassured her. "Let's just focus on staying healthy and not worry too much about things we can't control."

The doctor's words, though honest and practical, left us with a strange mix of unease and acceptance. They weren't exactly the comforting assurances we had hoped for, but they were grounded in reality. And while the uncertainty surrounding labour was something we couldn't control, Purvi was handling everything with ease and was enjoying getting pampered.

"Hey! You haven't taken me on a date yet," Purvi said, raising an eyebrow as we sat together one evening.

"Date? What date?" I asked, genuinely confused.

"The ninth-month date!" she replied, as if it were the most obvious thing in the world.

I blinked. "What?"

She rolled her eyes. "Arey, now couples go on a date in the ninth month—it's a thing!"

"Ohh," I nodded, catching on. "Okay, sure! How about tomorrow?"

"Really? Tomorrow?" she said, eyes lighting up—then immediately started murmuring to herself, "But what will I wear…"

The next day, we went to a well-known restaurant—NaCl. We ordered cheesecake and coffee. The food was okay, nothing too fancy. But honestly, it wasn't about that at all. It was about the moment, the laughter, and the little memory we carved out for ourselves in the middle of all the chaos. Just the two of us—on our ninth-month date.

And even though these days were passing slowly, it was time for our routine blood check-up, and as I stood waiting, I spotted Purvi coming down the stairs—just a little too quickly for my liking.

"Hey! Slowly! Watch your steps," I called out, half-worried, half-scolding.

The moment she saw me, she instinctively slowed down. "I *am* walking slow," she said with a mock frown.

"Yeah, right," I muttered.

We got the blood tests done, and later that day, the results came in. There was a slight dip in her haemoglobin levels. The doctor wasn't too concerned but advised us to make a few changes—add more beetroots to her meals, continue her medication properly, and most importantly, avoid stress.

Our evening walks after dinner had become a cherished ritual. Purvi, who once found it difficult to even manage short strolls, now proudly aimed for at least 5,000 steps a day.

"I feel lighter after these walks," she said one evening, looking ahead at the moonlit path. "It's like I'm doing something good for both me and the baby."

"But what about *me?*" I groaned dramatically. "Why do *I* have to walk 5,000 steps? The doctor asked *you* to walk, not me."

She looked at me, grinning. "You're the one who always says '*We are pregnant*'. And now you want me to walk all alone?"

I laughed. "Okay, fine. Let's head home now. Enough steps for today."

"No, no—one more round, please! Just the *last* one," she pleaded sweetly. "Let's go feed your cows. They must be waiting for you."

That had become a little ritual of its own—each evening, we carried some leftovers to feed the cows at the corner of the street. I genuinely enjoyed it. The cows would perk up and shuffle over the moment they saw me, and that little joy never got old.

Meanwhile, Purvi usually walked alongside, chatting away with her mom or relatives on the phone, her voice drifting in and out of the quiet night. These walks weren't just good for her—they became our calm in the middle of everything else, a peaceful pause.

Watching Purvi embrace these changes with such dedication filled me with pride and a hint of awe. The girl who once loved her lazy weekends had transformed into someone fiercely devoted, not just to herself but to the tiny life growing inside her. "Maybe this is what motherhood looks like," I thought to myself, marvelling at her evolution.

One night, during our usual post-dinner walk, Purvi suddenly turned to me and said, "You know... all these injections, blood tests, tasteless veggies, morning sickness, vomiting, cramps— everything just vanishes the moment I feel the baby's kick. It's a feeling I can't even explain. I don't think I would've ever done all this—eating healthy, exercising—if it were just for me."

I looked at her, silent for a moment, and smiled softly.

"Why are you smiling like that?" she asked, curious.

"Soon," I said, "there's going to be someone who will call your food *'Maa ke haath ka khana.'*"

She laughed, then shook her head. "But I don't even cook that well!"

"You're not that bad," I teased.

She narrowed her eyes. "You *should* have said, 'No Purvi, you cook *very* well.'"

I quickly tried to correct myself. "You cook very—"

"Not now," she said, cutting me off with a glance at her baby bump. Then, softer, more to herself, "Don't worry. I'll learn. I'll cook the best meals for my baby. And my baby's going to love it."

I leaned closer and whispered, "As if it'll have a choice."

She stopped mid-step and shot me *that* look.

"Just kidding," I grinned, holding up my hands in surrender.

We both laughed, and the night air felt just a little lighter after that.

The one thing we still hadn't figured out was a name for a baby boy. It wasn't because we hadn't tried. We already had a name picked out for a girl

- Reva. That one came to us easily. But for a boy? We had no clue.

At this point, it had almost become funny. Every day, Purvi and I sent each other reels and posts with baby boy name ideas. Things like "Top Boy Names of 2024" or "Unique Boy Names Starting With A or I." Instagram had basically turned into our baby name helper. The app kept showing us new names every time we opened it.

"Did you even see the reels I send you?" Purvi asked one evening, a hint of annoyance in her voice.

"I will, I will," I said with a guilty smile. "You send so many!"

"You never watch them," she said, pretending to be annoyed. "Anyway, look at this one." She held her phone up to me.

A cheerful voice in the reel said, "Top 10 Boy Names for 2024!"

"Advik... Aarush... Ishaan..." she read out loud. "What do you think?"

I gave a small shrug. "They're nice... but I don't know. None of them feel right."

Purvi sighed and leaned back on the couch. "You're no help. Don't know when we are going to find boy's name?"

I laughed. "Definitely before the baby is born."

"Haha" she said with a fake laugh.

I paused for a second, then asked with a smile, "But you are sure it's a girl, right?"

Purvi had made it very clear—she really wanted a girl. She talked about it all the time.

"I really hope it's a girl," she said softly. "Girls are just better, you know? They're smart, well-behaved, and fun to dress up. Don't you think?"

I smiled, already knowing where this was going. "Girls are great," I said. "But boys are fun too."

"Yeah, boys are nice too," she agreed. "But whether it's a boy or a girl... I hope the baby has your qualities. And your looks."

"That's true," I said with a shy smile. "I totally agree."

"But not your patience," she added quickly. "You're way too impatient."

I laughed again. "That's true. I was also actually born early, you know."

She looked at me, amused. "I'm not even surprised. But the fact that you are waiting nine months for this baby... now *that's* surprising!"

Our nights slowly started to revolve around baby name-hunting. With our phones in hand, we'd lie on the couch, scrolling through endless websites and apps.

"How about *Arin?*" Purvi asked one night, a little hope in her voice.

I looked up from my own screen. "Are we having the baby in the US now?" I joked. "What about *Kian?*"

She scrunched up her nose. "Sounds like *Gian.* I don't like it."

She thought for a moment. "Don't babies' names usually get picked by their *bua?* Should we ask Priya di to choose the name?"

"We can," I said, laughing, "but she'll probably be more confused than us."

Then she added, "Ruchi says she's going to call the baby *Pumpkin*—whether it's a boy or a girl. Says it works either way."

We both laughed, but deep down we were still stuck. No matter how many names we found, nothing felt *just right.*

A few days later, Purvi's mom called. As expected, the conversation naturally drifted to names.

"Why don't you pick something traditional?" her mom said. "Like *Arjun* or *Karan.*"

"They're nice, but they're too common," Purvi replied, shaking her head. "We want something different, something new and unique."

Her mom chuckled. "You kids these days and your obsession with being unique."

"It's the trend, Mom," Purvi said, half-joking. "Have you seen celebrity baby's names? *Raha, Abram, Vamika, Akaay*—so unique!"

Her mom laughed. "Then pick one of those!"

Purvi's eyes widened. "No way! Everyone will know we copied!"

As the days passed, the debate over the boy's name became less about finding the perfect name and more about enjoying the journey. We laughed at ridiculous suggestions, debated over meanings and origins, and even involved friends and family in the process.

But apart from names, there was one more important thing on our list—preparing the hospital bag. It felt like a big task, not just practically, but emotionally too. Packing that bag made everything feel real.

It was something we planned to do together, but our roles were pretty clear from the start: Purvi would make the detailed checklist, and I'd be the one to cross-check and actually get the items. Or at least, that was the plan.

"Okay, so what else should we pack?" Purvi asked one evening, sitting cross-legged on the bed, scrolling through her phone.

"See the reels I've shared with you," I replied, still glued to Instagram reels on my own screen.

Instagram had quietly become our go-to parenting guide. From baby must-haves to hospital bag checklists, almost every reel seemed to feature a cheerful mom-to-be, unpacking her perfectly arranged hospital bag.

After days of watching reels and my nagging, Purvi finally sat down with a pen and paper, dividing everything into two neat lists: For Mom and For Baby.

Reading aloud as she wrote, she began:

"For Mom:"

- Homecoming outfits

- Hospital outfits

- Nursing bras

- Maternity pads

- Toiletries

- Snacks

Then she moved to the next column.

"For Baby:"

- Baby clothes

- Swaddle cloths

- Dry sheets

- Carry nest

- Mosquito net

- Baby blanket

- Muslin napkins

"Is this everything?" she asked, handing me the list.

I glanced at it. "Looks good to me."

"You didn't even read it properly!" she said, raising an eyebrow.

"I trust you," I said with a small grin. "You've probably checked this twice already."

She let out a sigh—half amused, half annoyed—but didn't argue. "Fine. But don't blame me later if we forget something."

The next step was actually buying all the items on our hospital bag list. Thankfully, there was a store nearby that specialized in newborn essentials and maternity products. To make things even more fun, my mom and my sister Priya—who's always excited about shopping—decided to join us.

As soon as we stepped into the store, Priya's excitement was hard to miss.

"Oh my God, look at this tiny onesie!" she squealed, holding up a pastel yellow outfit. "It's *so* cute!"

"Oh yes, really cute," Purvi said, her eyes lighting up.

"Focus, guys," I said, smiling as I pulled out the checklist. "We've got a long list to get through."

The store was packed with things I had never even heard of: swaddle cloths, baby carriers, diaper caddies, and something called a baby grooming kit. It was a whole new world.

"What's a dry sheet?" I asked, picking up a pack and inspecting it.

"It's to protect the bed from... you know, leaks," Purvi explained, clearly in her element.

I nodded, trying to stay on track. "And this? Muslin napkins?"

"They're super soft cloths for wiping the baby. Very gentle," she said, adding them to our growing cart.

"Do we *really* need all this?" I asked, feeling a little overwhelmed.

Purvi gave me the *look*. "Yes. We do."

Meanwhile, Priya was off on her own little shopping adventure.

"We should totally get this sleeping bag too!" she said, holding up a plush pink bundle.

"Priya," I reminded her, "we don't even know if it's a boy or a girl yet."

"Fine," she said with a dramatic sigh, putting it back. "But I *am* getting this baby blanket. It's unisex!"

As the shopping bags started to fill, a quiet realization settled over us. This wasn't just about ticking items off a list anymore—this was real. This was our first real step toward welcoming our baby into the world.

Standing at the checkout counter, I turned to Purvi and said softly, "This is our first buy for the baby."

She looked at me, her eyes glistening with emotion. "Yeah... We're really going to be parents soon. It feels... surreal, doesn't it?"

Before I could respond, my mom smiled warmly and said, "You'll have a baby in your arms by next month."

Back home, the real work began—packing the hospital bag. Purvi laid everything out neatly on the bed, organizing each item with care and focus.

"Okay," she said, going through her list. "For me: clothes, nursing bras, toiletries—check. For the baby: clothes, swaddle cloths, dry sheets—check."

I stretched and let out a yawn. "Let me know if you need any help... I'm just going to take a quick nap."

Without looking up, she smirked. "You can double-check the bag once I'm done. Or you know, just pretend to check—like you did with the list."

I grinned, already lying back. "So no help it is then. But I know you'll do great. Good night!"

She shook her head, amused, as I pulled a pillow under my head for a quick nap.

As the bag was finally zipped up and placed neatly by the door, a wave of anticipation swept over us.

"So that's done," I said, stretching. "Now what's next on our to-do list?"

Purvi gave me a knowing look. THE BABY!!

The anticipation was everywhere. You could feel it in the air. It echoed in every room of the house, lingered in every phone call, and popped up in every single conversation: "When will the baby come?"

It wasn't just us waiting—everyone was counting down. Whether we were out for groceries or taking a quiet evening walk, people's eyes would always drift toward Purvi's growing belly. And like clockwork, the same question followed:

"How many months?"

Purvi had mastered her response by now. She'd offer a polite smile and say simply, "Nine."
But of course, that never ended the conversation. That's when the predictions began.

"Definitely a boy," someone would say with absolute confidence.

Sometimes she'd just smile and let it go. Other times, with a little sparkle in her eyes, she'd reply, "No, but I want a girl."

It happened so often that it became a part of our daily life. Cousins, aunts, uncles—even distant relatives and friends—no one could resist asking: "When is it happening?" As if Purvi held the answer to this great mystery.

One evening, as we were relaxing in our bedroom, Purvi leaned back against the headboard and placed her hands on her belly. She stared down at it with an exaggerated pout and said,

"Are you done enjoying in there? It's time to come out! When are you coming out, huh? Just come out already!"

I couldn't help but laugh at the sight of her mock-scolding her belly.

"Why are you laughing?" she asked, narrowing her eyes.

"Because you're overreacting," I teased, still smiling.

She gasped, dramatically. "*Overreacting?* I'm overreacting?".

She paused, staring at me. Then, before I could reply, her voice softened—but her words cut deeper.

"Everyone talks about the joy of becoming a mother... but no one talks about what a woman goes through to get there. Morning sickness, mood swings, bloating, backaches, swollen feet, stretch marks... the emotional rollercoaster. We sacrifice our sleep, our bodies, our careers, our identities sometimes. And yet, society just expects us to smile through it all — because we're 'blessed,' right?"

Her eyes shimmered, and her voice trembled slightly.

"It's not just about carrying a baby. It's about carrying the weight of expectations, fear, hormones, anxiety — all at once. And when we speak up about it, we're told we're 'Overreacting.' But why shouldn't we speak our truth? Pregnancy is beautiful, yes. But it's also hard. And women deserve to be seen, heard, and supported through all of it."

I sat there in silence, unsure of what to say—but feeling every word, she had just spoken.

A tear slipped down her cheek as she whispered, "I'm sorry... I don't even know what I'm saying."

I moved closer and gently took her hand.

"No, no... don't apologize. You're right. It *is* hard. But it's going to be okay. And soon we will have a beautiful baby with us."

She nodded slowly, wiping her eyes. "Hmm."

And in that quiet moment, filled with emotions we didn't quite know how to name, we simply sat there—together—waiting for the life we had created to finally arrive.

From that evening on, every little sign felt like it *could* be the moment. Every time Purvi felt a slight discomfort in her belly, my reflex was the same—I'd leap toward the hospital bag, ready to grab it.

"Is it time?" I'd ask, my voice a mix of excitement and panic.

"No, no," she'd say, her tone calm and composed. "Just a false alarm. Not a contraction."

"You're sure?" I'd ask again, clutching the bag like it was my lifeline.

"Yes, I'm sure," she'd reassure me, though a hint of amusement would play on her lips.

The cycle repeated more times than I could count. Each time, I'd ask, "Shall we go to the hospital now? Any contractions? Water broke? Baby coming?" And each time, she'd patiently shake her head no.

And with every false alarm, the anticipation only grew stronger. We were so close... and yet, not quite there.

As the due date crept closer, the waiting game only grew more intense. Nights felt longer, and the days seemed to stretch on forever. The air in the house carried a quiet tension—excitement mixed with exhaustion.

I'd often catch Purvi absentmindedly rubbing her belly, her gaze distant.

One afternoon, as she stared out the window, I asked softly, "What are you thinking about?"

Without turning, she said, "Why can't men carry the baby?"

I blinked. "What?" I said, half-laughing.

"I mean, it should be 50/50," she replied, completely serious. "First baby, the woman. Second one, the man."

I laughed. "Haha, I wish I were a kangaroo."

She turned to look at me, confused. "What?"

"In kangaroos, the males carry the baby... or something like that. Ah, never mind. It was a F.R.I.E.N.D.S reference."

She rolled her eyes, smiling. "Of course it was."

And just like that, the heaviness lifted—for a moment. We didn't know exactly when the baby would arrive, but we knew one weird animal fact.

Lately, Purvi had started talking to her belly more often. Soft whispers, gentle smiles—little conversations only the baby could hear. One evening, she looked over at me and said,

"Aman, come here—quick! Look at this!"

She grabbed my hand and placed it gently on her belly.

"Wow," I whispered, feeling tiny kicks against my palm. "I can feel them... our little one."

Purvi smiled, her eyes shining. "Yes, your little one is kicking so hard at me. Can you believe this?"
She paused for a moment, her hand resting beside mine. "It's amazing, isn't it? How even pain can feel like joy... when it's your baby."

Then she looked at me—softly, deeply.

"I don't think I can ever explain to you what it really feels like—to grow a child inside you. To hear its heartbeat before you even see its face. To feed it, protect it, nurture it... with your own body. That bond... It's not just emotional. It's physical. It's spiritual. It's everything."

Friends and family weren't much help either. Every phone call, without fail, began with the same questions:

"When's the due date?"
"How are you feeling?"

Purvi would reply with calm patience, every single time. "No, not yet," she'd say with a tired smile.

During a group video call one evening, Ruchi suddenly piped up, squinting at the screen. "Jiji, why don't I see any pregnancy glow on your face?"

"I was just about to say the same thing," Chirag, Purvi's brother, added with a teasing grin.

Purvi rolled her eyes dramatically. "Pregnancy glow is a myth, guys. When you're tired all the time, feel like peeing every five minutes, and your body is about to blow... the how can you expect someone to *glow?*"

We all burst out laughing.

Amid all the jokes and waiting, there were also moments of quiet vulnerability.

One night, as we lay in bed in the soft glow of the bedside lamp, Purvi turned to me and whispered, "Everything will be fine, right?"

"Huh?" I asked, caught off guard.

She hesitated before continuing. "We're almost at nine months, and I haven't felt any signs of labour yet. I just... I hope everything's okay."

I turned to face her and gently interrupted, "Hey, everything *is* okay. We just had a checkup last week, remember? And the doctor said there's no exact timeline."

She gave a small nod, but then admitted, "Yeah... but I checked on Google."

I groaned softly. "*Again*, Google? I told you not to search these things online."

There was a brief pause, and then I added more gently, "Look, it happens these days—lots of deliveries happen even after the ninth month. We still have a week to go. We've been having regular checkups, and the doctor knows way more than Google ever will."

She nodded again, this time a little more reassured.

One night, I noticed Purvi sitting up restlessly on the edge of the bed, fidgeting and shifting uncomfortably.

"What happened? Are you alright? Any contractions?" I asked, instantly alert.

She gave me a tired look and pointed to her belly. "Because *your* baby is in full-on play mode and thinks my stomach is a football. Just look at this!".

She grabbed my hand and placed it on her belly. "See? See how the baby's moving around? Uh! Not again..."

"What?" I asked, concerned.

"Pee. Again. Fifth time in the last hour."

I helped her up. "Hey, careful."

She waddled toward the bathroom, muttering over her shoulder, "And now here come the cramps too."

When she came back and sat down, I handed her a pillow to support her back.

"Just sit for a minute, breathe."

She leaned back with a sigh. "Yeah... I'm used to it now. I know I keep saying I want the baby to come soon, and for all this to be over—but..." She paused, a soft smile tugging at her lips. "Somewhere deep down, I think I'll miss this. Being pregnant. Being pampered."

I looked at her—hair slightly messy, eyes tired but glowing with something softer than light.

"You'll always be pampered," I said.

She smiled, resting her hand on her belly. "Let's see if you still say that after the baby arrives."

The ninth month was crawling to an end, and anticipation had become our constant companion. The doctor had set the estimated due date (EDD) for the 8th, but here we were, on the 6th, with no signs of the baby. Every movement, every twinge in Purvi's belly had us on high alert.

At our last appointment, the doctor had reassured us, saying, "If nothing happens by the 8th, we'll discuss whether to induce labour with medication or opt for a C-section." It was comforting to have a plan, but the waiting game was nerve-wracking. By the 6th, we were mentally and physically prepared for our hospital visit on the 8th, assuming that our little one was in no hurry to meet us.

On the morning of the 7th, I woke up to the soft rustling of movement. My eyes fluttered open, and I noticed Purvi pacing slowly around the room. It was unusual—she wasn't one to wake up this early, especially not at 6 AM.

"Purvi?" I called out groggily, rubbing the sleep from my eyes. "Are you okay?"

She turned to me, her face a mixture of discomfort and calm. "I think I might be having contractions," she said, her voice steady but tinged with uncertainty.

I shot up from the bed, suddenly wide awake. "Contractions? Should we go to the hospital? Are you sure?"

She gave me a small smile. "I'm not sure yet. Let's wait a bit and see if they're consistent. It might just be false labour."

I could see she was in pain, though she was trying her best to downplay it. Despite her discomfort, there was a sparkle in her eyes that hinted at the incredible moment we might be on the brink of experiencing. I couldn't help but smile.

We decided to monitor the situation for a while. I anxiously sat beside her, watching her every move.

"Is it bad?" I asked gently as she sat on the edge of the bed, her hand resting on her belly.

"It's manageable," she replied, wincing slightly. "It's not like what they show in movies—at least not yet."

I chuckled nervously. "Well, let me know when it starts feeling like a Bollywood movie."

She rolled her eyes but laughed despite herself. "No PJs please".

As the minutes passed, the contractions began to feel more real. They were still spaced out, but there was no denying their presence. By 7 AM, we decided it was time to inform our families.

We went straight to the kitchen. Mom was doing her usual morning chores when I walked in, trying to stay calm—but my voice gave me away.

"Mummy... I think it's happening," I said, my tone a mix of excitement and nerves.

She turned instantly, eyes wide. "Really?!" she exclaimed, her whole face lighting up. "I *knew* it would be today—I just had a feeling!".

She rushed over to Purvi. "Purvi beta, how are you feeling?"

"Not too bad," Purvi said, trying to stay steady. "The contractions are coming and going."

"Stay strong, okay?" Mom said, placing a hand on her shoulder. "Let's get ready for the hospital and see what the doctor says. I'll quickly make some halwa."

She hurried out to the hall to tell Dad, and I could hear the excitement in his voice too.

I turned to Purvi and asked, "Don't you want to inform your mom?"

"Let's first see what the doctor says," She replied. "Once we know for sure, I'll call."

By 8 AM, the contractions were more frequent, though still bearable. Purvi decided it was time to take a quick shower and get ready, "just in case."

She double-checked the hospital bag, even though she'd already done so a dozen times.

"Clothes, check. Clothes for the baby, check. Documents, check," She muttered to myself, ticking off items on an imaginary list.

When Purvi emerged, she looked calm and collected, though I knew she was bracing herself. "Ready?" I asked.

"Almost," she said.

"Let's eat something before heading to hospital." I said.

Mom was bustling around the kitchen. True to her word, she was making halwa. The smell of roasted Halwa and ghee filled the house, creating a comforting atmosphere.

"Here, have some," she said, handing Purvi a small bowl. "It's for strength. You'll need it."

Purvi took a bite and smiled. "It's delicious, Mummy. Thank you."

The morning started with a whirlwind of emotions as we prepared to head to the hospital. Purvi, despite her contractions, seemed unusually calm, her face serene yet determined. As we left for the hospital.

"I have one request," she said, her voice light but resolute.

"Anything," I replied immediately, ready to do whatever she needed.

"I want a *Motichoor* laddu," she said.

I blinked, caught off guard. "Right now? Like, before we go to the hospital?"

"Yes," she nodded firmly. "I really need one. Please."

I hesitated for a moment. "But Purvi, you're having contractions. Shouldn't we get to the hospital as quickly as possible?"

She gave me a playful glare. "Listen, I'm the one in pain here. If I can wait for the baby, you can wait for a few minutes. I'm not going to the hospital without my laddu."

Her determination left no room for argument. With a small chuckle, I said, "Alright, alright. Laddu it is. Let's find a sweet shop."

We stopped at a nearby sweet shop. I rushed inside, explained the urgency, and came back with a small box of *Motichoor* laddus.

"Your highness," I said, presenting the box to her dramatically.

She laughed, though it quickly turned into a grimace as another contraction hit. "Thank you. It's very yummy."

With the laddu craving satisfied, we finally made our way to the hospital. By this point, Purvi's contractions had grown stronger and more frequent. As we walked into the doctor's clinic, her grip on my arm tightened.

The doctor greeted us with a warm smile. "So, how are we feeling?"

"Contractions are stronger," Purvi said, her voice steady but strained.

The doctor immediately got to work, checking her vitals and examining her. After a few minutes, she looked up with a reassuring smile.

"Everything looks great," she said. "The cervix is 2 cm dilated, which is a good start for a normal delivery. You're having a baby today!"

Purvi and I exchanged a glance, our faces lighting up with joy. "Today?" I repeated, as if needing confirmation.

"Yes," the doctor said. "Go home, gather your things, and get her admitted. Also, here's a little help to speed things up."

She handed me two small bottles of castor oil.

"Mix this with tea or milk and have her drink it," the doctor instructed. "It helps with dilation."

On our way to the hospital, Purvi picked up her phone and called her mom.

"Maa... it's happening!" she said, her voice a mix of excitement and nerves.

"Today?!" her mom gasped on the other end.

"Yes."

There was a pause—just long enough to feel her mother's joy even through the silence.

"I'm so happy, beta. How are you feeling?"

"I'm okay, just some contractions," Purvi replied. "Also, please inform Ruchi."

"Yes, yes—we will. We'll be there soon, okay? Take care and stay strong, beta."

Back at home, while Purvi rested on the couch, I unscrewed the cap of the castor oil bottle, a pungent, unpleasant smell hit me. I instinctively wrinkled my nose.

"Wow," I muttered, holding the bottle at arm's length. "This stuff smells horrible. Are you sure you can drink this?"

Purvi, sitting calmly despite the contractions, gave me a determined look. "If it helps for normal delivery, I'll drink it."

I mixed the oil with some warm milk and brought it to her. "Here you go," I said, handing her the cup cautiously.

Purvi took the cup, examined it for a moment, and, to my utter astonishment, downed it in one go.

I stared at her in disbelief.

After taking the castor oil, we busied ourselves with packing the hospital bag—adding all the last-minute essentials we might need.

Suddenly, Purvi winced and grabbed her belly.

"Ouch!"

"Another contraction?" I asked, quickly moving toward her.

She nodded, breathing through it. "Hmm... a big one."

"Okay, just sit down for a minute. I'll check the bags one last time."

She lowered herself onto the edge of the bed, still holding her belly.

"I'll also go change—let me wear something more comfortable for the hospital."

"Okay, but walk slowly," I said gently, watching her closely, heart pounding just a little faster.

An hour after Purvi bravely drank the castor oil, its effects began to show. She had been pacing the living room, trying to distract herself from the growing discomfort, but now her steps slowed.

She stopped, leaned against the wall, and clutched her belly. Her face twisted in pain.

"Purvi, are you okay?" I rushed to her side, concern surging through me.

She gave a small nod, but her frown deepened. "The pain... it's getting stronger."

"Okay, okay—just a little more time. We're going to the hospital. Let me check if Mom and Dad are ready."

I ran to the hall. Dad was already outside, getting the car ready, while Mom was on a call with Priya.

"It could happen anytime now," I heard her saying. "Just try to catch the next train if you can."

"Mummy, we have to leave now!" I called out, voice urgent.

She turned quickly, nodded, and spoke into the phone, "Okay, Priya, talk to you later—we're leaving now," and hung up.

She grabbed her dupatta and slipped on her sandals. "Let's go."

As I helped Purvi into the car, another contraction hit. She clutched my hand, her grip like iron.

"We are almost there," I said, trying to sound calm even as my heart pounded.

With a deep breath, Dad started the car.

As soon as we reached the hospital, Purvi's cries of pain became sharper and more frequent. The moment the staff noticed her condition, they immediately brought a wheelchair and whisked her towards the OT. I ran alongside her, clutching her hand tightly until we reached the doors.

"Don't worry everything will be good," I said softly, though my voice wavered.

And just like that, the doors shut, leaving me standing there with a mixture of anxiety and excitement.

Barely a moment had passed when my phone buzzed. It was Ruchi, Purvi's sister, who couldn't make it due to work commitments but was brimming with curiosity and excitement.

"Jiju! What's happening? Is she in labour?"

"Yes, they've taken her to the OT," I replied, trying to keep my voice steady.

"Oh my God! Is everything okay? Did the doctor say anything?"

"They said it's going well, and we can expect a normal delivery," I reassured her.

"That's such a relief! Please keep me updated every second, okay? I feel so helpless being far away!"

"Sure" I promised.

The waiting area outside the OT felt like an eternity. I paced back and forth, glancing at the clock every two minutes. My phone vibrated occasionally with texts and calls from either Ruchi or Priya.

At one point, I tried peeking through a small glass window in the OT doors, but a nurse firmly guided me back. "Sir, please wait outside. We'll let you know as soon as there's news."

"Is everything okay inside?" I asked, my voice almost pleading.

She smiled kindly. "Yes, everything is progressing well. Don't worry."

Despite her reassurance, I couldn't help but feel restless. I began asking every nurse or attendant who walked out of the OT for updates.

"How's my wife?" I asked a young nurse who came out carrying some instruments.

"She's doing fine," she replied, clearly used to anxious husbands. "It'll take some time, but everything is under control."

Each bit of information was a lifeline, but the minutes dragged on like hours.

Soon, more family members began arriving. Yogesh Uncle walked in, followed by Pratik and Ridhima, cousins who were equally excited and curious. Their arrival brought some much-needed distraction.

"Any news?" Uncle asked as he approached me.

"Not yet, but the doctors said everything looks good," I explained.

"Good, good," he nodded, visibly relieved.

Ridhima sat next to me, her eyes sparkling with excitement. "Bhaiya, what do you think it'll be? A boy or a girl?"

"What do you want?" I replied with a small laugh.

"Boy," she declared confidently.

Pratik chimed in, "I think it'll be a girl."

The guessing game continued, with each person making their predictions. It was amusing to see how invested everyone was in the baby's gender, though I chose to stay neutral.

Just as I was lost in thought, another nurse walked out of the OT. This time, I was quicker.

"How is she now?" I asked urgently.

"She's progressing well," she said with a reassuring smile. "The baby will be here soon."

The words "baby will be here soon" sent a jolt of excitement through me. I quickly texted Ruchi and Priya, letting them know the latest update.

The hours had felt like days. Every tick of the clock seemed to stretch endlessly, as if time itself was holding its breath.

We had been clinging to the hope of a normal delivery. The doctors had reassured us again and again—Purvi was strong, she could push through. But then, the door opened, and the doctor walked out, her expression serious. And in that moment, the ground beneath us shifted.

"What do you mean, Doctor?" I asked, my voice barely steady.

She met my eyes calmly but firmly. "She's given it everything she has, but her strength is starting to fade. The baby's head is larger than we anticipated, and it's become stuck. It's making it extremely difficult for her to push."

She paused for a beat, then added, "We'll continue monitoring for a little longer, but we may need to intervene."

The air in the waiting area changed instantly. All the light chatter, the hopeful guesses about the baby's gender—it all fell silent. Even the walls seemed to be holding their breath.

My mom, ever the calm in the storm, stepped forward.

"Doctor, may I go in to see her?" she asked. "I'll sit with her for a few minutes, give her some strength. Maybe seeing me will help."

The doctor hesitated, then nodded. "Alright. You can go in—but just for a few minutes."

I watched as my mom entered the OT, my heart thudding in my chest. he seconds dragged. Every creak of a door, every passing nurse made me look up, hoping—willing—for good news. Every time my phone buzzed, it was either Ruchi or Priya.

"Bhai, what's happening now?" Priya's voice carried a mix of excitement and growing worry.

"The doctor says it's becoming difficult," I replied, trying to sound calm, trying to stay hopeful. "Mummy is with her now."

"What? But she was fine just a while ago!"

"It's the baby's head," I explained, the words catching in my throat. "It's larger than expected... it's stuck. It's making it really hard for Purvi to deliver normally."

There was a pause on the other end.

"Oh... everything will be fine, Bhai. Just keep me updated, okay? Let me know what the doctor says next."

"I will," I said, ending the call.

I sat back in the chair, staring at the closed doors. My hands were cold, my chest heavy. In that moment, all I could do was wait—and hope.

When my mom finally emerged, her face was pale, her composure shaken. My heart sank.

"What happened? How is she?" I asked, standing up abruptly.

"She's exhausted," my mom said, her voice barely above a whisper. "She's tried so hard, but she's almost unconscious. She can't push anymore."

"What? But how? She was doing fine earlier!"

"The strain has been too much. She's lost a lot of energy. The doctor says it's risky to continue trying for a normal delivery."

I clenched my fists, frustration bubbling over. "I need to see her. I can make her respond. She'll listen to me. Please, let me go in."

Seeing me helpless Mom requested the Doctor and she agreed. "Alright, but only for a moment. She's in a fragile state, and we need to make a decision soon."

As I stepped into the OT, the stark reality hit me like a punch to the gut. Purvi lay on the bed, pale and almost unrecognizable. Her hand was stained with blood, her face devoid of its usual glow. For a moment, I froze, unable to process the sight in front of me.

I forced myself to move closer, my heart breaking with every step. I placed my hand gently on her forehead.

"Purvi," I said softly. "It's me. I'm here."

Her eyelids fluttered weakly, but there was no response.

"Purvi, you've come so far," I continued, my voice thick with emotion. "Just a little more, and we'll meet our baby. I know you're tired, but you're the strongest person I know. One more push. Just one."

But she remained unresponsive, her body too weak to fight any longer.

The doctor placed a hand on my shoulder. she said gently. "We need to move to a caesarean. Waiting any longer could be dangerous."

I nodded reluctantly. "Do whatever it takes to keep them both safe."

When I returned to the waiting area, the family looked at me expectantly. Their hopeful faces made it even harder to speak.

"The doctor says a caesarean is the only option now," I said, my voice heavy with emotion. "Purvi is too weak, and continuing the normal delivery would be too risky."

Dad placed a comforting hand on my shoulder. "You made the right decision. The important thing is that both Purvi and the baby are safe."

Everyone nodded in agreement, though the tension in the room was palpable. Ruchi called again, and I explained the situation to her.

Ruchi said, her voice quivering. "Everything will be fine."

"Hmm" I replied, hanging up and sinking into a chair.

The wait resumed, and the minutes felt like years. Every time the OT door opened, my heart skipped a beat, only to be met with nurses carrying equipment or hurrying past.

Finally, after what felt like an eternity, a nurse stepped out of the OT, her face lit with a warm smile.

"You can come in," she said, looking at me.

Mom and I hurried inside, our hearts pounding with anticipation.

As we entered the room, the doctor looked up with a smile. "Congratulations—it's a girl! Both mother and baby are healthy. Purvi is currently resting in other room."

The moment I heard *"girl,"* all the noise and chaos faded away. It all melted away.

There she was, wrapped in a soft pink cotton cloth, lying peacefully under the warm glow of the light. My breath caught in my throat. I took a slow step forward.

She was perfect!

Her tiny eyes fluttered, half-open, half-closed. Her face—so pure, so delicate—it didn't feel real. Her tiny hands moved slowly, and her little feet twitched ever so slightly. I reached out, hesitant but drawn. As I touched her, her little fingers curled around mine—light as air, soft as silk. She was more than anything I could have ever asked for, and far more divine than I had ever imagined. Had I been able to freeze that moment, I would have relived it a hundred times over— each minute, each second drawing me deeper in love with her.

My vision blurred—my eyes heavy, my chest full of something too big for words.

That first touch... it was magic.

(In my heart)
Purvi, our girl has arrived. You were right. It's a girl—the most beautiful girl in the world.

REVA has arrived.